Secret Sacrifices

Cynthia L. Hall

PublishAmerica
Baltimore

First printing

ISBN: 1-4241-7257-8
PUBLISHED BY PUBLISHAMERICA, LLLP
www.publishamerica.com
Baltimore

Printed in the United States of America

This book is dedicated to Karen and Randy, who keep my imagination flowing.

Dear Mrs Hillstad,

I hope Secret Societies gives you hours of pleasure reading. It's a thriller, so you might want to wrap up in a blanket in a cozy chair before you get started!

Enjoy!

Cindy

I wish to thank the Wadsworth Writers Group, Freda, Jan, Mary and Jenny for all their support and hard work with helping this project become reality. Thanks to everyone at PublishAmerica for supporting and believing in your authors.

July 4, 2005

Tracey felt the cold wet cloth pressed hard against her face, fully covering her mouth and nose. A sweaty hand gripped her arm. She tried to twist free, but a ten-year-old's strength is no match for an adult's. She felt dizzy and sick to her stomach. Then everything went dark.

Hours had passed when Tracey awoke lying on an uncovered lumpy mattress of a twin bed frame. Her feet were bound together and tied to the footboard, and her hands were tied separately to the posts of the headboard. Frantic for her mother, she searched the room but found she was alone. The room was dark from the heavy drapes that were pulled closed allowing only a small beam of light to show through the gaps on each side.

Panic washed through her as she recalled what had happened. She and her mother had been standing along the roadside watching the St. John Independence Day Parade floats creep by. Tracey had joined the other children running into the street to collect candy, noisemakers and other trinkets the people threw from the floats. A clown walking beside one of the floats tossed out handfuls of deflated balloons. Tracey stooped to get a florescent green balloon from the ground. Just as she was about to pick it up, it moved two feet in front of her. She walked to it, and when she tried to snatch it, the balloon was jerked away from her grasp. She laughed, looked up and saw the clown pulling the string that was tied to the balloon. They repeated the game five more times until the clown disappeared into the crowd along the roadside. She could still see the balloon, and when she stopped along the edge of the crowd to get it, she felt the large arms grab her and felt the rag against her face. Now, far removed from that moment, she could recall hearing the shouts from her mother to come back.

Tracey's thoughts were brought back to the present with the smell of bread baking coming from the other side of the closed bedroom door. The aroma reminded her of many Saturday nights when she and her mother had made bread and soup and Tracey started to whimper. Spontaneously, she gritted her teeth to stop from crying. Her tenacity was synonymous with her red hair, the same shade that she had inherited from her mother. And even though she felt afraid, she was not going to allow herself to lose control; she would be strong like her mother.

Looking around the room, she noticed its tattered and worn condition making her feel more uncomfortable. The faded flower printed wallpaper was peeling off in many spots exposing the bare wall. Tartan drapes hung over the tall window across the room from the bed. Only a few drapery hooks held the pleats to the rod, leaving sagging gaps along the top. Unstained wooden floor planks, never varnished, bore a dark path from the bed to the door. The bedroom door opened slowly. Tracey wanted to scream, but her chest felt tight and she couldn't breath. The light from the room beyond made it possible for her to see only the small shadow moving toward her. Tears streamed down her face. As the shadow came closer, she saw it was a child, a little girl with hair to her waist.

"Evita! " A man with a deep voice called to the girl. The little girl turned sharply and ran out of the room, leaving the door cracked open.

"Wait," Tracey blurted. But the girl was gone. Tracey stopped sniffling to listen and strained to see beyond the open door.

On the other side of the door, seven-year-old Evita ran to the lady standing at the kitchen sink known as Mama. Evita grabbed Mama's skirt, wrapping herself inside. The woman gently patted the small child's shoulder.

"There, there now. You know the rules."

Evita shook with fear as Mama's husband, Mister Killbane came toward her. All the children living in the house feared Mister.

"Mama, leave go of her," he ordered. "Evita, come here."

Evita peeked around the side of Mama's skirt. Two other children stood silently at the kitchen table, waiting for the Mister's wrath.

Chapter 1

Maggie Brown stepped off the plane and felt the warm tropical breeze brush gently across her face. For a moment she wanted to embrace the pleasant feeling the wind gave her, but couldn't muster any good feelings since Tracey's disappearance. Without her daughter by her side, Maggie dreaded returning to the island. Many times as she thought about that horrid day when Tracey disappeared, she wondered what she could have done to make things turn out differently. She took pride in the fact that, as a single parent, she watched her daughter as well as any two-parent family. She and Tracey traveled often, without any problems, and a small place like St. John in the U.S. Virgin Islands was not at all intimidating. St. John was not a haven for criminal activity, and the trip should have been a smooth one.

She shook off the thought and went about business. As previously planned, Maggie's first task was to rent a Jeep and meet Matt Sanford in the cemetery on the other side of town. She hadn't wanted to call Matt, but she had to do everything possible to find Tracey. After all, Maggie had been the one to break away from their relationship, and although she was sure Matt must harbor bad feelings, she felt that Matt's law enforcement training could help find Tracey. Maggie had taken the search into her own hands when she grew impatient with the authorities, thinking they were moving too slowly. She was desperate and knew Matt was her only hope.

Maggie's job at F. J. Fowler's Art Gallery in New York City was to seek out new artists from all over the world and set them up for an exhibit at the gallery. Flying globally and renting cars came with the territory. Usually there was nothing special about rental vehicles, but the vehicles on St. John were different. She looked forward to driving the four-wheel drive Isuzu Jeep, which made it easy to move around on the mountainous terrain.

Three months ago, when she and Tracey had made the trip, they enjoyed unsnapping the plastic windows and folding back the convertible top. They had laughed when Maggie forgot about driving on the left side of the road and rounded one of the hairpin turns only to find they were heading straight on with another Jeep. Most of the time the people in the other vehicles were tourists also and would cheerfully point to the proper lane. Maggie smiled while remembering how she and Tracey would put an imaginary checkmark in the air with their fingers when they were able to do the same to another set of vacationers.

Chapter 2

As Maggie approached the rental facility, she repeated over in her head the fictitious name that Matt had instructed her to use. Matt had explained to Maggie that the two of them would work undercover, telling only St. John's police chief, Juan Otiga, about the plan. The Chief had been instrumental in helping Maggie look for Tracey and had become her friend.

"Since you don't know how long you'll be staying, Mrs. Watkins, we can hold your deposit and we will settle the bill when you return the Jeep." The plump red-faced lady handed the keys to Maggie over the counter of what looked more like an ice-cream stand than a rental office.

Maggie took the keys and managed a fake smile, something she was getting good at, masking her true feelings. What she really wanted to do was scream, scream at everyone. Why hadn't Tracey been found? Why weren't the police doing more? Maggie hated giving in to her emotions. She had worked hard for years to always appear in control, convincing everyone near her that she was independent and confident. After Tracey's disappearance, she let her anger empower her to give her the strength she needed to keep going. On the drive to the cemetery, Maggie took a deep breath and forced back tears.

Right after Tracey had been taken, Maggie spent hours with the FBI and the local police going over every detail of that day. That's when she and Chief Otiga had become good friends. He helped her to repeat over and over again exactly what she could remember.

It had been the fifth day of their vacation. They awoke at seven, ate breakfast, and talked about the day. On that particular day their plans had been made in advance of their trip. There are only two small towns on the island, Cruz Bay and Coral Bay Village. Cruz Bay was having the annual town festival held on Independence Day, which included a parade.

People from all nearby islands came to visit St. John for its festivities. Stores and restaurants closed for the duration and reopened when it was over; everyone participated. Entrants dressed in the most colorful clothing available and walked along the route singing, juggling, and playing native instruments. Maggie and Tracey had known they would be attending the parade, and before they left New York they made costumes in bright oranges, yellows and shades of green. Each of them wore ruffled skirts and halter-tops made from lightweight cotton and accessorized with beaded necklaces. Tracey's skirt was short and tight and Maggie's was ankle length and split up the side to her thigh.

Wearing such a scant outfit was not customary to Maggie, who had become more familiar in the past years with a conservative business suit. Each time Maggie was made to recall the event, she smiled as she remembered what Tracey had said. "We look like the lady with the fruit on her head. What's her name?"

"You mean Carmen Miranda," Maggie answered. And each time Maggie was forced to tell the story she could barely choke out the words, remembering Tracey's sweet laughter. When they arrived in town they had found everyone similarly dressed. The vivid colors made the tropical island come alive. As beautiful as it was, it was also that same costuming that had abetted in Tracey's abduction.

Chapter 3

The last time Matt Sanford had seen Maggie was at their college reunion eleven years earlier. They had broken up right after Maggie's graduation and Matt had attended the reunion hoping to see her again. They had eaten dinner together and danced every dance. Maggie had even gone back to Matt's apartment and stayed the night. He thought they had united as a couple once again after that night. He was so sure of it that he had purchased an engagement ring the next day. Maggie was gone from his apartment when he returned home and would never return his calls. When he made an effort to see her at home, she would either not answer the door or wasn't there at the time. He tried contacting her at work, but found her friends covering for her by saying she wasn't available. Matt understood then that Maggie had no desire to rekindle their relationship. He kept the ring and hoped for an opportunity to persuade her in the future.

After several months had passed he realized he should have returned the ring. Years later he saw her in a restaurant in the city and thought about going over to say hello, but decided it wasn't a good idea. If Maggie had wanted to see him she would have made contact.

"Excuse me, sir, we'll be landing soon. I need to take your tray."

Matt was deep in thought and startled by the stewardess. He smiled and handed her the tray. Her perfume lingered as she walked up the aisle of the plane. It reminded him of the first time he had seen Maggie.

Her body was wet from the pool and smelled of roses. His sister was on the high school swim team and Matt went to congratulate her while she and her teammates stood in a huddle after a race. He saw Maggie standing with his sister and was interested immediately.

From a distance, Matt noticed Maggie's long slender legs, accentuated by her high-cut swimsuit. When he stood close beside her, she looked up at him and the brightness in emerald green eyes stood out against the white purity of her skin. A cluster of freckles huddled around her nose.

"Welcome to St. Thomas." The pilot was making announcements as they landed. "The weather is normal for October. The high today is 87 degrees, the low tonight 77 degrees. Winds are out of the south with a chance of a quick shower. If this is your first time visiting the island, and you are caught in a storm, you'll find they hit hard without much warning. The storm is usually a torrential downpour that lasts about five to ten minutes. After that the sun will shine the rest of the day. Please remain seated until the airplane comes to a complete stop and enjoy your stay."

St. Thomas Airport in Red Hook didn't have air conditioning. To compensate, many large windows were left open. Matt looked around for the luggage turntable and noticed the airport hadn't changed since he had been there years earlier when he and his family came to celebrate his parent's 30th Wedding anniversary. The airport looked more like a worn out garage than an airport. He grabbed his luggage and went to find a cab. The cabs on the island were much different from the large Plymouths and Chevrolets in New York City. Islanders drove small foreign makes and models that were in poor condition. Matt eyed the selection and settled for a worn out two door Fiat. He held his hand up to hail the driver.

"Do you have other bags, sir?" The driver spoke the native English language with a Jamaican dialect.

"No, just these two." Matt hadn't been sure how long he'd be on St. John, so he had crammed as much as he could into one medium duffel bag. He had brought along several pieces of equipment and carried them in a shoulder bag.

"Where to, mon?"

"I'm looking for the ferry to St. John."

"Get tin. I will have you there in a jiffeh."

"Ferry to St. John, ferry to St. John." An older couple stood in front of the line of cars, yelling to the drivers.

"Over here. I con take you to de ferry." The driver flagged the couple to his cab.

The couple came running, holding several pieces of luggage. "Oh, thank heaven. We thought all the cabs were taken and we would have to wait," huffed the out of breath woman.

The driver opened the small trunk for their bags. He loaded the couple's bags first, then stuffed Matt's duffel bags on top. The lid barely closed. The couple squeezed into the back seat, filling the small area. The front of the car held two individual bucket seats, and when Matt sat down, he did so with a thud. The springs were shot and it felt like he was sitting on the vehicle's floor. Matt's height made it hard for his legs to fit between the dashboard and his seat.

"All aboard," said the cabby. As he pulled away from the curb, it started to rain.

The passengers hurried to roll up their windows. It was hot outside and the tiny car didn't have air conditioning. In a matter of seconds the windows steamed and made it impossible to see through them. With each winding turn, the couple in the back seat was tossed from side to side, their plump bodies gently smashing against each other.

"Oh dear," laughed the lady. "Can you see where you're going?"

"Ya, miss," answered the driver.

"Mrs. Smith," she introduced herself. "And this is Mr. Smith."

"Just a little rain, Mrs. Smith," continued the cabby. "We are used to dat here on St. Thomas."

Matt was lucky to have a small, but extremely useful handle on the dash in front of him. He held on as the car made sharp turns.

"Is this your first time on the island?" Matt looked over his shoulder to the Smiths.

"Oh, no. My wife and I come every year. I'm a retired banker and you know how hectic that can be." He and the missus looked at each other and giggled.

"We come here to get away from our busy life in St. Louis to get, ah—you know—laid back." Mrs. Smith's round body jiggled as she laughed. "When we first came seven years ago, we stayed on St. Thomas. Every time we visited, we explored the other islands. For the past three years we've been committed to St. John. It has the most beautiful beaches and the people are friendly."

The lines around the cabby's eyes drew together as he smiled. Matt caught Mr. Smith glancing at the driver in the rearview mirror.

"What Mrs. Smith means is that *all* the islands have friendly people."

"Oh, Mr. Smith, you know what I mean." She playfully slapped her husband's ample arm. "Anyway, where are you headed, Mr…" Mrs. Smith asked Matt.

"It's Watkins, and I'm going to St. John on business. My sister vacations here often and has always raved about one of the restaurants. I own a restaurant in New York and I thought I'd check it out for myself. If I like what I taste, I'm prepared to offer the chef a new job."

Mrs. Smith's appeared interested. "Which restaurant is it? We might know it."

"Bon Appétite." Matt had done his homework of the island and knew what to say, and since his days as a private investigator he was used to telling small fibs when needed.

"Yes, we know it." Mrs. Smith seemed proud to know the place. "You remember the place, Mr. Smith."

Matt thought it was cute they called each other by their proper titles, yet it was no surprise to him because they seemed the type.

"In fact," she continued, "we've eaten there several times. We always get a table so we can see outside. It has a gorgeous view of the park and sits on the side of a mountain. You can see straight down. They boast of having the best view on the island. Remember, Mr. Smith?"

Mr. Smith rubbed his chin in thought.

"You eat prime rib or breaded lamb chops there," she reminded him.

Mr. Smith lifted his eyebrows. "Oh, I remember. Great beer too."

The cabby wiped clear an area in the windshield. It seemed the defrosters weren't working. But as worn as the small auto was, this was not a surprise. Matt hoped they didn't have much farther to go. The humidity was starting to raise the temperature in the car as well. He debated between keeping the window up and staying hot and dry, or rolling it down and being cooler and soaked. He opted for the former. The driver stopped short, forcing all three passengers to brace themselves as they flew forward.

"We have come to de ferry," he announced. "Dat will be ten dollars each, please."

Matt reached into his rear pocket for his wallet. He withdrew fifteen dollars and handed it to the driver.

As the cabby took the money from the Smiths, he looked up at the sky through the windshield. "Looks like we all gonna get wet now." He smiled to his passengers and opened his door to exit.

Matt followed, holding the newspaper he had read on the plane over his head. As he grabbed for his luggage in the trunk, he found the newspaper of no use. The downpour had completely soaked through.

As the Smiths took their luggage, it was as if someone had turned off the faucet and the rain stopped instantly. The sun popped out and the steam began to rise from the road.

Taking the conditions in stride, the cabby pointed to a twenty-eight foot boat at the docks. "Bettah hurry. I tink dats your boat getting ready to shove off now."

"Oh, dear," exclaimed Mrs. Smith. "We'll have to wait a half hour if we can't catch this ferry."

Matt glanced toward the boat and saw that the ropes that held the boat to the dock were being untied. Without hesitation, he ran toward the dock, the

Smiths trailing behind. Mrs. Smith was taking two steps to each one of the men's long strides.

One of the boatsmen waved nonchalantly to the captain. The captain nodded in response and the boatsman motioned for Matt and the Smiths to come aboard. They leaped on board and the boat moved away from the dock. The Smiths rushed to the only open area at the back of the boat.

Matt looked around the full boat and spotted a flat metal surface in the front. It wasn't really a seat, but it was enough for him to sit. Rainwater dripped from his clothing and the water caught in his thick black hair ran down onto his face and into his eyes. He was carrying his bags and wasn't able to wipe his face until he sat down.

Once situated, Matt noticed the worn condition of the metal boat. It was painted a pastel blue, but years on the water had nearly stripped away all signs of color. What was left was raw metal and patches of rust.

The dark-skinned captain looked to be in his fifties and seemed more worn than his boat. Matt suspected from his looks that he was a man who probably knew the sea and the boat that he captained. His two boatsmen, also natives of the island, were younger, but seemed experienced as well.

In his research, Matt had read the ferry ride took about twenty minutes. He took the opportunity to look around and get his bearings.

Since the rain had stopped, the sky was pale blue and scattered with large white billowing clouds. The boat was moving at a good pace, which made the clouds look as though they were moving smoothly across the sky. As St. Thomas became smaller in the distance, St. John became larger. The air was clean and salty.

Matt took a deep breath through his nose, filling his lungs quickly. He blew out the air slowly through his mouth. After he had repeated the breathing ritual several times, a wave of calmness washed through him and he began collecting his thoughts. It was then that Matt realized he was anxious about seeing Maggie again. He was also anxious to find her daughter, but feared the worst. Tracey might already be dead. Missing children cases often close in one of two ways; the children are found alive and abused, or their dead bodies are recovered. Each scenario could be as traumatic as the other, and he was not going to inform Maggie about either.

Chapter 4

Maggie drove to the restaurant across the street from the cemetery. Ellington's was Tracey's favorite place to eat on the island. She parked in the parking lot and walked across the narrow road to the cemetery. It was the Chief's idea to meet at the cemetery because Matt had asked for privacy. The cemetery was just outside of Cruz Bay and didn't have much traffic. Maggie glanced at her watch and expected Matt to be on the island soon. His plane was to land on St. Thomas around eight o'clock. She had offered to meet him at the docks, but he had insisted he meet her this way and said he'd explain when he saw her.

As instructed, Maggie walked to the center of the small graveyard to wait. The deceased residents on the island were placed in coffins and entombed in cement cases above ground. She guessed there to be about one hundred on the two-acre area. It wasn't hard to locate the middle of the property.

She brought her cell phone so she could call Chief Otiga and tell him she was there. Two rings in, Maggie got an answer.

"St. John Police Department." The woman's accent was prevalent.

"Is Chief Otiga there, please?"

"He is out right now. Con I take a message?"

"Yes, this is..." Maggie remembered Matt's instruction, tell no one you are there–only the Chief. "Ah, no thank you. When do you expect him?"

"I tink he should be bac in an hour. He went to de hospital."

"Is he alright?" Maggie thought something might be wrong.

The woman laughed. "Oh, yaw. He is all right. He went to pick up a pacage."

Relieved, Maggie told the dispatcher she would call back later. She chuckled when she thought how different things were on St. John compared to New York, or any big city. Islanders were carefree and volunteered information. An NYPD dispatcher wouldn't be so generous with information.

Maggie checked her watch again. She was looking forward to having Matt with her—to help find Tracey. Matt was always so sure of himself, so strong and self-reliant. He would be the strength she lacked. She thought all his cloak and dagger instructions odd, but she also trusted him. He had enough experience on the force that she was sure he knew what he was doing.

Maggie looked up in time to see a taxi pull into Ellington's parking lot. Matt exited the front seat, passenger side, and closed the door. He leaned in the open window of the small car to pay the driver. He was wearing khaki shorts, a navy blue polo shirt, a tan ball cap, socks and running shoes. Even with his sunglasses on, Maggie made no mistake identifying him. *He's as handsome as ever*, she thought. A sudden rush of excitement waved through her, making her feel uncomfortable and anxious. *Stop it,* she thought. *I hate this. Why am I so upset? Get a grip, girl.*

Matt walked toward the restaurant until the driver was out of sight, then turned and headed her way. He was more muscular than when she had last seen him—so many years ago. Maggie always kept control of her emotions and always conducted herself in a professional manner, but she was struggling to remain composed now. Her heart began to race as he came nearer. She began to panic. This was not like her. *What should I do? Take his hand and say, nice to see you. Hug him? After all, we did live together.* She became annoyed with herself for feeling like a schoolgirl again. Flashbacks of seeing Matt for the first time were fresh in her mind. The sun was setting behind him as he crossed the street and the glow lit up the cemetery like a stage. Maggie stood paralized in center stage. "Matt." She managed to blurt out his name.

"Red, you're looking well under the circumstances." He held out his hand and she grabbed to meet his shake. Matt's one-sided grin that had once melted her heart made her feel at ease. "Have you spoken with the chief yet?"

"No, I just called a few minutes ago and he was out."

"It doesn't matter. We have plenty to do while we wait to meet with him."

He took her elbow and swung her around, walking toward the back of the graveyard. "Let's get out of sight."

"Really, Matt, is all this stuff necessary?"

He stopped abruptly, swung her around so they stood face to face. "Listen, Red. I'm not trying to scare you, but I mentioned this when we talked on the phone. If I'm going to help find Tracey, you're going to have to trust me, and you're going to have to follow my instructions all the way—and to the letter. Got it?"

Maggie was annoyed with his tone and instantly felt the blood rise to her face.

"Yes, I understand," she answered sharply, and yanked her arm from his grip. "But know this. If I question what you say or do, I will be asking questions and I will be entitled to some answers. I am not a five-year-old who doesn't understand or care about what's going on around her."

Matt's dark brown eyes sparkled as his grin reappeared. "Still the same old headstrong Red, eh?" He continued walking, with Maggie following. Once they reached the back of the property, Matt checked her mood. "We wait here. Any questions yet?"

She purposely didn't answer. He set his duffel bag on top of a grassy area and sat on one edge. He patted the other with his hand. "Here, sit down."

Maggie obeyed, but only because she didn't want to sit on the ground. She was aware of St. John's day critters, as well as its night critters, the island home to many small lizards running about.

Matt opened his carry-on and took out a large over-stuffed file folder. "I'm not sure how much you know about the island, but in the next few days you'll know more than anyone who's lived here all their life. I've made arrangements with a local woman to rent a house on the south side of the island while we're here."

"Why the south side? Tracey was taken from town."

"We don't want anyone to know you're here and looking for her. That's most important. That's why the alias, and I have an ID for you that matches that name. Tomorrow we'll do something about that hair of yours. You stick out and you need to blend in."

"Color my hair?" she raised her voice.

"Yeah, and you'll be getting it cut too."

He had taken her by surprise with that notification and she missed what he said next.

"Right?" he asked.

"What did you say?"

"I said I won't be able to call you Red anymore." Matt laughed.

"Ah, very funny." She bumped his arm with her elbow and smiled. For a moment Maggie felt relaxed. She had forgotten what that was like. Each day Tracey was not with her she had grown more tense, until she felt tight all over.

He winked at her and continued. "My assistant has put together a complete history of the island, including maps and locations of surrounding islands."

"Since when do police officers have assistants?"

"I quit the force four years ago and have been doing private investigating. I thought you knew that."

"No, I didn't. When I called the police department in New York and asked for you, all they said was they would have you call me. They didn't tell me you weren't there any longer."

"I still have great connections there. They won't volunteer any information to outsiders."

Maggie took offense to his remark. She was certainly no outsider in Matt's life. After all, they had loved each other and lived together. Even though she realized what he meant, she didn't care for his choice of words.

"We'll pick a small secluded beach and spend some time covering that white, freckled body of yours. You'll need a tan to go with your new do. And while you're basking in the sun, you can study this material." He handed Maggie an inch thick folder.

"I don't see how I can sit on a beach somewhere while Tracey could be taken farther away from me."

"Really, Red." Maggie could hear the importance in Matt's voice. "We need to do this. You need to look like you belong on the island and you need to know every inch of it like your own hand. Once we are in that position, we can go anywhere and talk to anybody about anything. People will talk to us then, tell us what they know, what they've seen. Right now you're a stranger to them and everyone here. And what do we teach our children?"

"Not to talk to strangers." Maggie stared at the ground and didn't bother to hide her disappointment.

He put his arm around her shoulders. "I want to find her as much as you do—and we will. Okay?"

Maggie wanted to snuggle close to Matt. She wanted to give in to her emotions and sob like a baby. She wanted to let Matt be the strong one, let someone else do all the worrying. But she only let herself glance at him and managed one of those fake smiles she had learned to give.

The sun slipped down behind Ellington's Restaurant giving way to the night sky. Shades of pink, blue and gold reflected upon the ocean water. Moored sailboats dotted the bay water along the town's banks. Maggie's eyes rested upon Gallows Point, a group of vacation rental units that sat tucked into the curve of the bay in the tiny town of Cruz Bay. The last time she and Tracey had eaten at the Ellington's, they had talked about staying at Gallows Point on their next trip.

Chapter 5

Mr. and Mrs. Smith didn't have time to unpack. They had a job to do, and it needed to be done tonight. As usual, they didn't meet the person who hired them; they only spoke with him on the phone. He had referred to himself as the Cuban. All the arrangements were made with just one call. Half of the money was wired before the hit to a Western Union in Miami near where the Smith's lived, and the other half would be left in their motel room when Chief Otiga was dead. The Smiths charged the Cuban double the usual amount because a police chief was a high profile mark.

Unlike the story they told Matt, this was their first trip to the island. In their line of work, their own existence relied on one lie after the other, and they were good at it. They took every precaution to ensure a clean hit and their anonymity. Their makeup and disguises made them look ten years older, appearing to be about seventy. They were masters of disguise after so many years in the business.

"This is a beautiful island, Mr. Smith," announced Mrs. Smith. "Do you think the cabby and the restaurateur bought our story?"

"Hook, line, and sinker, Mrs. Smith. After all, we are experts at what we do."

"Mr. Smith, you flatter me." His wife laughed.

Mr. Smith opened the closet door in their motel room where the extra linen sat upon the shelf. The shelf was too high for him to reach, so he used a chair to stand on and removed the two bed pillows that sat to the edge of the shelf. A loaded Browning Autoloader .22 caliber rifle was pushed to the back, just where the Cuban had said it would be. Mr. Smith specifically asked that it be loaded and told the Cuban no extra ammunition would be needed. He only intended to take one shot.

"Right where he said it would be," he said. "Bring me the ski bag, dear."

Mr. Smith pulled off an envelope that was attached to the rifle barrel with tape. Together they placed the gun into the bag and stuffed towels around it. They sat on the edge of the bed while Mr. Smith opened the envelope and pulled out the note that was inside.

"Let's see where our target is," he said. "It says Chief Otiga will be at the St. John's Hospital from 7:30 to 8:30. After that he will be going home."

Mrs. Smith looked puzzled. "How would our client know exactly what time our mark would be where?"

Mr. Smith patted his wife's hand. "Really, dear, you know the fewer questions asked the better off we are. I didn't ask, but my guess is whoever gave us this information must be close to the chief. Close enough to know when and where he'd be tonight anyway. We'll just work from the information we've been given. Do you have the chief's address?"

"Yes, I wrote it in pencil in my book that I read on the plane. Don't worry, when we're done tonight, I'll erase it.

"Always thinking. That's what makes you so good." The two chuckled.

"We better get going, Mr. Smith. Time's a wastin'."

They locked the motel door behind them and went to their rented Jeep. They kept the canvas top on the Jeep, making it hard for anyone to see inside. They didn't want to take any chances.

Chapter 6

Maggie pushed the off button on her cellular phone. "The chief will be here in a few minutes. He's just leaving the hospital."

"So how well do you know the chief?" Matt's question was asked with a bit of sarcasm.

"Enough to have spent several nights with him."

"Is that right?"

"He took me under his wing through the FBI's investigation. The FBI men were nice enough, but very regimented and matter of fact. The chief saw how intense things were and invited me to dinner one night."

"And how old is *our* chief?" Matt lifted an eyebrow.

"*Our* chief, as you put it, is a married man with two young children. His wife, Janice, asked me to stay with them while I was here. They both thought it would be better for all of us, especially since the chief and I were working so closely together. In fact, they wanted me to stay with them this time, but you had different ideas."

"That was nice of him and his wife to offer, but as you said, I do have another plan."

A car came up the road and the two of them leaned behind the grave they were sitting next to so they wouldn't be seen. It passed by. They could see the headlights of another car coming around the bend from town. This time the car pulled into Ellington's lot and Chief Otiga got out. Maggie stood, waited until he started across the road, and started to walk toward him. Matt grabbed her arm.

"Wait. Let him come to us."

A bit miffed, she stopped as Matt had said. She wondered if he was trying to scare her on purpose. As the chief stepped onto the cemetery property, another car was rounding the bend. Matt pulled Maggie to the ground, but the chief kept walking.

"Gee, Matt. You're too jumpy."

"Just trying to be cautious, Red."

"There's cautious, and then there's paranoia," she rebutted.

Matt's grin said it all. Maggie stood to greet the chief.

Chapter 7

"He pulled in there." Mrs. Smith pointed to Ellington's lot.

Mr. Smith drove around the next bend. He shut off the lights to his vehicle. "I wonder where he's going?"

"There's no traffic. This might be our chance, dear."

Mr. Smith agreed and pulled off to the side of the road, just past the cemetery property into a wooded area where no houses or buildings were visible. There was just enough bend in the road that only the glow of the lights from Ellington's could be seen.

"I noticed there weren't many cars in the lot at the restaurant. Hopefully, there won't be any traffic."

"If we hurry, we'll be done and gone before anyone comes. Get the bag, dear. Let's get to work."

Mrs. Smith handed the ski bag to her husband. He made his way through the wooded area while she positioned herself in the driver's seat and waited.

"Maggie, it's good to see you." Chief Otiga hugged her.

"And you too. Chief. This is Matt Sanford."

"Hola, Mr. Sanford, nice to meet you." The two men shook hands.

"Please call me Matt."

"Sí, and you can call me Chief." He laughed.

"I like a man with a sense of humor." Matt grinned. "We can have a seat here if you'd like?"

"Por favor, please. That will work."

Maggie and Matt found their seats while the chief leaned against the graveyard tomb. "I have some important information for you. One of the shop owners stayed in the day of the parade to do paperwork. He was standing by his door taking a break and could see the back of the crowd watching the parade. He noticed a clown that matched your description, and a child that matched Tracey's description, come through the crowd and walk down the street a block. They got into a brown pickup truck. He said what caught his eye was the clown was carrying the girl. It didn't mean much to him, but he thought it was funny she had fallen asleep during all the excitement."

Maggie's stomach turned. Tracey wouldn't—wasn't asleep. How could he have been carrying her? She would have been struggling to get away.

"Did he get the make of the truck?" Matt asked.

"He didn't see the whole truck. He could only see the back of the bed of the truck. It was parked in the alley facing away from the street. He didn't see them get into the cab of the truck, but they were only out of sight for a minute, then he saw the clown throw his bag of balloons in the bed of the truck. Seconds later, they drove away."

Maggie was speechless. This was the first time anyone had come forward to say they had seen them together. She sat motionless, listening to the two men talk.

"I have one of my men at headquarters working with the shop owner trying to get a make on the vehicle. It was only yesterday that this information was discovered, but we are running all the plates on all the brown pickups we see. We haven't found anything suspicious yet."

"Do you have a year in mind?" asked Matt.

"We think it must be an older model. The shop owner believes the truck had mucho rust. He wasn't sure because of the brown color."

The chief took Maggie's hand in his and patted it. "Maggie, this is good news. It's a small lead, but a lead nonetheless. It's a step in the right direction, and I am very hopeful. We can go over everything tomorrow."

Maggie held the chief's hand and looked up at him, trying to appear hopeful. She heard a cracking sound from the woods and turned her head toward the noise. Without warning, the chief's hand was ripped from hers as he fell backward onto the ground. Blood oozed from his forehead.

"No " screamed Maggie.

Matt grabbed Maggie, throwing her to the ground beside him. "Stay down!" he shouted. He lifted his head slowly to look around, but it was too dark to see anything in the distance. Matt crawled on his belly over to the Chief. He checked for a pulse on the chief's neck. The chief lay dead on the ground with his eyes still open.

"Stay here," Matt said. He got up and headed toward the woods. Matt used the cement tombs as shields, darting from one to another, making his way to the cemetery's edge. Although only one shot was fired, there was a probability that more than one person could be waiting in the woods.

Mr. Smith had knelt on one knee to steady himself for the shot. When he tried to get up, he caught his pant cuff on an exposed tree stump that tripped him to the ground. The rifle flew from his hand, landing just out of his reach. He rolled on his stout belly, stretching as far as he could to get the gun. Dragging it back with his fingertips, he used the rifle as a crutch to stand on his feet. Mr. Smith hobbled as fast as he could through the woods.

Mrs. Smith had started the engine of the Jeep when the gun was fired. Even thought the Jeep was a rental, turning on the headlights was prohibited so that no one could see the plates. She held a flashlight out of the driver's window with the light beam showing on the ground in an effort to be a beacon for her husband. It was a perfect night, with the warm air blowing gently, but Mrs. Smith perspired. Mr. and Mrs. Smith had talked many times about retiring. They were getting too old for this sort of thing. The light of the flashlight captured Mr. Smith limping toward her.

Matt ducked behind a tomb when he heard the woods come alive in front of him. He was on the very edge of the cemetery property with the cut-off line made by palm trees and jungle-like foliage. He heard heavy breathing and grunting and thought one or two men might be engaged in some sort of scuffle. He listened intently, peeking above the tomb and peering into the darkness of the woods, unable to see any movement.

When he heard footsteps, he took off after them. At this point, he could hear only one person running away. He plunged ahead, hoping no one was waiting behind a tree. His eyes had adjusted to the dark some, but he was still unable to see whoever was out there. With outstretched arms, he used his hands to help guide his way through the woods. He followed the sound of the footsteps, estimating them to be at least one hundred yards away. The thinned out area of palm and fir trees was no problem to move through quickly, but the rocky ground underneath slowed his pace. Matt's foot landed hard on a rock, twisting his ankle, but he kept going.

A dim light in the distance caught his attention. He saw it flickering and in the next moment he saw the interior lights of a Jeep go on. He thought he could see two people in the front seat, but he was too far away to recognize them. In another instant, the vehicle sped away, spraying sand behind its wheels. Since there were no streetlights, and no lights on the Jeep as it drove away, Matt was unable to get the color of the Jeep or the license plate number.

Mr. Smith hopped into the passenger's seat of the Jeep, throwing the rifle in the back. His wife's book fell onto the ground. "Let's go," he told his wife. He panted like an out of breath dog and held onto his leg.

"Are you okay?"

"I'm alright. Just drive. We're far enough away now, you can turn on the lights."

She turned on the vehicle's running lights and looked at her husband in the light from the dashboard. He was sweating and had sand stuck to his skin from rolling on the ground.

"Oh my. We *are* getting too old for this nonsense."

Mr. Smith's heart rate was beginning to recede and his breathing was slowing to normal. He gave a deep sigh of relief. He looked up just in time to see headlights coming right at them.

"You're on the wrong side of the road " he shouted.

His wife swerved the Jeep to the left side of the road just in time to avoid a head-on collision.

"That was close," she said. "I forgot about driving on the left."

Mr. Smith chuckled. "I guess you are right, dear. Retirement here we come. I think we'll consider this our last job."

"Oh, thank Heaven," answered his wife.

Chapter 8

Maggie lay on the ground beside the deceased police chief where Matt had left her. She heard him exit the wooded area, but couldn't take her watery eyes from the chief.

"It's okay now, Red. You can get up." He helped her trembling body to stand.

"How could this have happened? And why?" she asked.

Matt began gathering his gear. "I know you're not going to want to hear this now, but we have to go."

"What?"

"We can't stay here."

"We have to stay here— and wait for the police."

"I don't know if whoever did this saw us or not, but we're not sticking around so they can read about us in tomorrow's paper. For all they know, we might have seen them." He started for Maggie's Jeep. "Come on."

Maggie's feet felt like they had been glued to the spot. She couldn't take her eyes from the chief—from her dead friend.

Matt walked back and took Maggie's arm, pulling gently. "Come on. We can't do anything for him now."

It seemed to her at that moment that this was not the Matt she remembered. The Matt she remembered would have stayed and taken care of the matter at hand. He would have called and waited for the police to come and helped them find the killers. He had changed, and she was afraid she had made a mistake in calling him.

She forced her feet to move, but she was still shaking in shock. Visions of the chief's wife and sons ran through her mind. How would they ever handle this? They would be alone now. Alone like she was, without Tracey. It was a lonely, horrible feeling, and she felt sorry for the Otigas.

There still wasn't any traffic on the road and only two cars in the restaurant parking lot, probably belonging to the staff. Matt threw his bags in the back of the Jeep and opened the passenger door for Maggie. She got in without a word. He ran around to the driver's side and hopped in.

"The keys?" he asked.

She reached into her short's pocket and pulled out the key. Her hand shook uncontrollably as she handed the key to Matt. He started the Jeep and left the parking lot, but didn't turn the Jeep's lights on right away, escaping in the dark, then turning them on a short way down the road. Maggie numbly stared ahead. The top was down on the Jeep and her red hair blew wildly in the wind.

"Where are we going?" she asked.

"We'll check in at Turner's beach house. There's nothing more we can do tonight."

They rode the rest of the way in silence.

Chapter 9

Claire Turner had been expecting them. She usually met her clients with the company taxi and would escort them to a Jeep rental. Then she would lead them from the rental facility to the vacation unit. This time the guests were coming to her. Claire owned property all over the island and had a sister company on St. Croix. She had come to the islands when she was twenty years old and had fallen in love with the ambience. She borrowed money to buy the first unit, then took the next five years of scrimping to fix it up enough to rent. During that time she had stayed in an efficiency apartment. After one year of renting out *The Sundance*, she mortgaged that property to buy another, eventually owning fifteen properties on both islands. It had proven to be a very successful business decision for her over forty years ago.

Matt had a friend on the police force who had vacationed through Claire many years and knew she could be trusted. He had explained their circumstances and she was sworn to secrecy. Matt had studied the map on the plane and was able to follow the directions Claire had given him easily, even in the dark.

Claire was standing on the deck that overlooked Coral Bay below when she heard them coming. As with all her properties, this one was built on the hillside with a beautiful view. St. John's mountainous terrain made it possible to build houses hidden in the hills and viewable only by water. This house, in particular, was well out of sight, even from the road above. A wooden sign with the name *Bayview* carved into it stood by the entrance, and was the only marker to show a house existed. A small light in the ground next to the sign made it possible to read in the dark.

Matt pulled in and followed the twisting driveway covered with huge green foliage to the home's back entrance. Claire appeared through the sliding glass doors.

"Welcome to the Bayview." Claire's smile diminished when she looked at Maggie.

"Hello, Claire. I'm Matt Sanford and this is Maggie Brown."

The new guests looked exhausted and disheveled.

"Nice to meet you," she said, as she and Matt shook hands. "You must be tired after the trip."

"You have no idea," answered Matt.

"Then I'll just show you a few things about your rental and be off."

Maggie went to a chair overlooking the deck and sat down. She hadn't uttered a word, or even looked at Claire. Claire showed Matt around the two-bedroom, two-bath house.

"I did the grocery shopping as you asked and put things away in the kitchen. Do you want me to show you where things are stored?"

"No, thanks. I'll find them." Matt grinned at her.

"Here are the keys, and if you need me, my number is on the bulletin board beside the phone. Just call and I'll get anything you need." Claire put her hand on Matt's arm, leaned in and whispered, "Is she all right?"

"She'll be okay. She's been through a lot today. Thanks for all you've done and I'm sure I'll be calling."

Claire left without another word. Matt went to the galley-style kitchen and opened cupboard doors and took out the chamomile tea Matt had asked Claire to purchase along with a list of other groceries. He remembered Maggie once liked it. He put water in the kettle on the stove and placed a tea bag into a cup.

Matt backed up against the cupboards with the dark gray countertops and crossed his arms against his chest. Their accommodations weren't the Ritz or AAA. The appliances in the kitchen were twenty years old and, as with most rental units, they had gotten plenty of use. The pine cupboards were painted white enamel to give the kitchen a contemporary look.

The linoleum floor sported large black and white squares with the official flower of the United States Virgin Islands, the Yellow Elder, painted on several of the white squares. The bright yellow flowers lit up the room. Claire's decorating skill made her rental units different from others, and kept people coming back year after year.

The rotating ceiling fan lent a small breeze in the windowless room. To the left of the kitchen was the great-room, a combination living room and dining area. Looking into the room made it easy to see why people came there. The only separation between this area and the outside were two walls of sliding glass doors. The doors were open with the screens pulled across, letting the trade winds blow through the house.

The teakettle whistled. He brewed the tea and delivered it to Maggie. "Here, drink this."

"I don't want any." She waved him away.

"I'll set it on the coffee table in case you change your mind."

Maggie sat motionless in a scooped bamboo swivel chair. She had the chair turned toward the screen door and gazed into the night. The warm breeze blew across her face. She turned herself around to see Matt, who sat on the overstuffed leather couch that faced her. He had his feet propped on the coffee table in front of him.

"What do we do next?" she asked.

Matt noticed the change in Maggie's shell-shocked face. Frowning with confusion, he replied, "Next?"

"Where do we go from here?"

"What are you? Some kind of Jeckyl and Hyde?"

"Jeckyl and Hyde?"

"Moments ago you were in shock and full of grief."

"I still am. I have been for the past three months." She paused and continued sarcastically. "You know—since my daughter was taken from me." She reached for her tea. The cup rattled against the saucer as she sat back in her chair. She used her right hand to steady them. Matt could see how hard Maggie was working to appear unshaken, and decided not to tease her anymore.

"Tomorrow I'll call the police station and talk with the officer the chief has working the case."

"And the chief?"

"I'm not going to cover my disappointment about that. I was counting on him to help. But now, we'll do it ourselves."

"Was he killed because of us? Because of me?"

"Possibly." Matt walked to Maggie and took her teacup from her, placing it on the table. He knelt in front of her. "This was not your fault. He's a police chief."

"*Was* a police chief."

"That's not the point. It's the nature of the job. His death could have been related to this case or it could have been related to a case from ten years ago. The point is, he put his life on the line every day. That's what he chose to do, and that's why he's dead. Not because of you."

Maggie knew in her heart that was true. She just couldn't help thinking, if Tracey hadn't been kidnapped Juan Otiga might be on his way home to his wife and children.

"I'm going out to get the rest of our luggage. Yours in the back of the Jeep?"

Maggie nodded her head, then finished drinking her tea. When Matt had gathered all the luggage, they went to the rooms they had selected to unpack. Maggie turned on the clock radio that was on the night stand next to the bed. The sounds of a steel drum band played through sporadic bits of static.

She unpacked short-sleeved cotton blouses and hung them in the small walk-in closet. Maggie was a slight build, wearing only a size five, which allowed her to pack several pairs of shorts, pajamas, undergarments, shoes, two dresses and a bathing suit into one large suitcase. She wondered why he had instructed her to bring her suit. After all, what good would that be in finding Tracey? But she learned tonight that she would be wearing it first. She had packed her cosmetics in a carry-on, which she took to the attached bathroom to unpack. Just as Maggie was putting the last piece of clothing away, she heard the radio announcer break in.

"We interrupt our program for this news just in. The police chief of St. John has been fatally shot tonight. We repeat—Police Chief Juan Otiga of the Island of St. John has been the victim of a shooting tonight. We'll bring you the full story on our eleven o'clock news this evening. This is WRRA Radio 1290 from St. Croix..."

Maggie pushed the off button on the radio and sat down in the high-backed wicker chair beside her bed. She put her face in the palms of her hands and cried for Chief Otiga, his family, and herself.

Chapter 10

Counting Tracey, there were nine children living in Mister and Mama's house. In three month's time, Tracey had learned a lot from the other children. She learned all the children had been kidnapped, and she learned to do what Mister said or suffer the consequences. Some of the children who caused trouble disappeared. The two oldest children, fourteen-year-old Nalda and twelve-year-old Teodoro, had become good friends with Tracey. When each of the children had arrived at the house, they were given a Spanish name and told to memorize the meaning of that name. Nalda's real name was Erin and Teodoro's real name was Michael. Tracey was given the name Leonora.

Nalda and Teodoro looked after the younger ones and tried their best to keep them safe from Mister. Mister had a terrible temper, and if the children didn't listen they would be punished by being put in the disobedient box that he had built in the barn. Tracey learned that Mama hated the box, but was obedient to Mister, too.

Teodoro had made a list of each of the children's names, new and old, so they wouldn't forget who they really were. Each child carried a list in their pockets during the day and kept it in their pillows at night. Tracey pulled her list from her pillow every morning and read it before getting dressed.

Age When Kidnapped	Age Now	Real Name	New Name	Meaning
3	12	Michael	Teodoro	Gift from God
6	14	Erin	Nalda	Strong
3	10	Pamela	Freiza	Sister
5	11	James	Moises	From the water
5	10	Christa	Juana	God's gift
4	8	Erick	Tobias	God is good
10	13	Cody	Jose	God will increase
2	3	Rachael	Evita	Eve
10	10	Tracey	Leonora	Light

Each year the children changed their age on their birthdays. Some of the children were too young when they were taken to know their birthdays. Their age was changed each Christmas, the only holiday they were permitted to celebrate. Mister and Mama do not allow the children to celebrate birthdays, so the children did it in hiding.

"Tracey, you better put that away and get to the kitchen. Mama's starting breakfast and needs our help," Freiza told her as she left the bedroom.

Tracey stuffed the list in her tattered denim shorts and looked around the room to make sure little Evita had made her bed. The five girls slept in one room and the four boys slept in another. Mama and Mister were extremely strict about keeping things in order, and Tracey didn't want anyone to get in trouble.

They lived on a farm in an old farmhouse with many rooms. Everything in the house was old and worn, but nothing was out of place or dirty. The children did the cleaning and helped Mama with the cooking. There were chickens, pigs, two Dobermans, many cats and a large garden on the farm. This farm was different from the farms Tracey had seen in New York. Tracey had no idea where she was, but she thought the farm looked something like St. John because the ground was sandy and rocky. It didn't have the dark dirt like home, and the trees were similar to the ones she had seen on the island. None of the children had any idea where they were, or how they got there.

Jose had been kidnapped and brought to the farm when he was ten years old, three years ago. When he was eleven he tried to escape. Waking early one morning, he got up and snuck away. He walked hours in one direction, never seeing anyone. Jose crossed two dirt roads and ended on a sandy beach. All he could see from the beach was water. He told Tracey he wondered if he should have taken one of the roads.

Mister found him, beat him and brought him back to the farm in his truck. He beat him again with his belt and put him in the box for a week.

Mama came to the box every day with food and water. Each time she would say, "You don't run away again, okay?"

He and none of the other children ever tried to escape after that.

The boy called Tobias was so afraid of Mister that he did everything he was told. He had been kidnapped four years ago when he was four years old. He was a rambunctious, independent four-year-old and used the word "no" often. He spent many nights in the box, but amused himself in the small dark area by creating stories in his mind, and by carving on the walls with a sharp rock.

One night, when he was six, he refused to go outside to collect wood for the kitchen stove because it was storming. Mister put him in the box for two days. On the second day the storm became a hurricane, flooding the farm and the house. The box filled to the top with water. The water pushed Tobias to the top of the four-foot high area. He found a small corner where the water topped off and formed an air pocket, and he was able to float and breathe.

When the worst of the storm had passed, Mama made her way to the box and found Tobias gasping for air, frightened beyond repair. Tobias became a different boy on that day and never did anything wrong that would land him in the box again.

Tracey went into the kitchen and started working right away. Today was Thursday and on Thursday mornings they ate scrambled eggs and fried potatoes. The potatoes were kept in the pantry in a bin on the floor. There weren't many left and it was Tracey's duty to add items to the grocery list. She gathered twenty potatoes and placed them on the counter. She then went to the refrigerator and used the hanging pencil to put potatoes on the list. This was one of the few times writing was permitted, and Tracey was one of three children allowed to write. She, Nalda and Jose were the ones to take care of the written word. Tracey and Jose figured out it was because of how old they were when they had been kidnapped. Since they already knew how to read and write, they were picked for the job.

Mama and Mister weren't aware of Teodoro's literary ability, so he was not asked to do that chore. He was only three years old when he was kidnapped and Mama and Mister thought they had molded him well, keeping him from learning. But Nalda and Jose had taught him to read and write, and were teaching the others also.

Three-year-old Evita had become quite attached to Tracey. She followed her everywhere, and Mama was jealous of Tracey because of it. Although Mister always enforced the punishment on the children, they were plenty afraid of Mama too. After all, they had been kidnapped so Mama would have children.

Evita was a scamp of a child with long flowing blond hair and huge round blue eyes. She always hid in Mama's skirt, and would cuddle close to her in the evenings after all the work was done for the day. But that was before Tracey came to the farm.

"Evita You go on outside now and feed the chickens. Tracey can do the potatoes herself," Mama ordered.

Evita looked up at Tracey and put out her bottom lip. Tracey nodded to go ahead and Evita did as she was told. It was a good thing Mama was standing at the sink with her back toward them or they both would have been in trouble. The older children felt Mama liked the younger ones better. They thought Mama was afraid of the older children because they were getting older and smarter. Teodoro liked it that way too. Someday he would use that to his advantage. He felt it was the children against the adults and taught the others to feel that way too.

When Teodoro first met Tracey, he asked her what day it was. There were no radios or televisions on the farm and Mister and Mama wouldn't tell the children, telling them it didn't matter. Teodoro double-checked to see if Tracey's information matched with his last confirmed calculations, and he was proud to find he was right. Tracey was taken on a Tuesday, the Fourth of July and by his calculations that would mean today was Thursday, the nineteenth day of October.

Tracey carried the potato peelings outside to the compost pile in the field, just behind the barn. There she found Teodoro staring beyond the field. "What are you doing? If they see you standing here doing nothing, you'll be in trouble," she fussed.

He showed Tracey a picture frayed around the edges with creases across the front. "I think this is a picture of my parents."

"Where'd you get it?"

"I've had it with me since I was taken. I've hidden it all these years."

Tracey looked at the faces in the picture. "You look like the man."

"That's why I'm pretty sure it's my parents. I found it on the bedsprings in my room many years ago." He took the picture from Tracey and stuffed it in the pocket of his shorts.

Tracey saw how sad it made him.

"I've been thinking," he continued. "Except for Evita, we're all old enough to outrun Mister."

"And?" She was afraid of what he was going to say next.

"And, if we sneak out during the night, we can make it to the sea by early morning." Teodoro was planning to escape and take the other children with him.

"What about the dogs?"

"That's what I've been thinking about. When Mister kidnaps the kids he uses something on a rag that makes them fall asleep, and maybe it will make the dogs sleep too." He turned to look at Tracey. "I'm almost finished with the raft, and I know it will float."

"Do you have the stuff that will make the dogs sleep?"

"That's where you come in. You and Nalda will have to find it. Look everywhere. Kitchen, basement, bathroom, everywhere."

"What do you think it looks like?"

"I'm pretty sure it will be a liquid of some sort. Nalda has permission to go almost everywhere on the farm. She can look in places you're not allowed to go."

"What do we do about Evita?"

"She's little, and she loves you. She'll follow you anywhere."

Tracey smiled.

"It's Tobias I'm worried about. I don't know if we can get him to go."

Tracey was suddenly aware of the time that had passed. "I can't stay outside any longer. I have to get back to the house. I've been gone too long now." She dumped the peelings on the pile and ran for the house.

Teodoro continued to stare across the land he soon would walk across. In the distance he could see the Dobermans running the perimeter of the property. Since Tobias had attempted escape, Mister had bought the dogs for the farm to keep people out and the children there. If the children so much as raised their voices in play, the dogs would bark at them. He would have to do something about the dogs to get by them and escape.

Teodoro heard a noise in the barn and knew it was Mister looking for him. He scrambled back into the barn through a hole at the bottom of the barn siding. He placed the two bales of hay back in front of the hole and ran to the horse stall nearest to him. In the nine years Teodoro had been on the farm, he had never seen any horses. The stalls were used to house supplies for the farm. Teodoro hid his half-built raft above the stalls in the hayloft, behind the old unused bales of hay.

"Teodoro, get the slop ready and feed the pigs " ordered Mister.

All the other children answered Mister with, "Yes, sir." Teodoro was defiant, and chose to say nothing, and chose to push Mister to his limit. He was determined to make his getaway plan work and save the other children, no matter what he had to do.

Although he had only known Tracey for three months, he knew he could count on her help. She was much like Teodoro and was determined to get back to her mom.

Inside the house, Tracey and the rest of the girls set the table and cooked breakfast. The entire time Tracey's mind raced about what Teodoro had told her. It was very dangerous to look for the liquid and she knew if she was caught something worse than the box might happen to her. She didn't want to put the other children in danger, but she trusted Teodoro and Nalda. She felt they were smart beyond their years and thought it was because of the responsibilities put upon them growing up with Mama and Mister. The two had a bond beyond brother and sister, and Tracey felt lucky to be included.

She was also terrified of Mister. All the children were forbidden to wander around with nothing to do and had to have a definite purpose for being where they were. Tracey was afraid to search for the liquid and was hoping Nalda would offer to do most of the searching.

Ten-year-old Juana was helping to set the table when Mister came into the kitchen.

"Mama, is breakfast ready yet? I have to get to work!" he shouted.

The force of his voice startled Juana. She turned sharply, dropping a dinner plate. It shattered into a hundred small pieces on the floor. Mama, Tracey, and Juana froze momentarily in their spots. Mama broke the silence by walking toward the broken glass.

"There now, Juana. You get the broom and I'll start to clean up."

Mister held his right hand up to stop Juana. "Tracey will get the broom. Juana, you come with me." Mister stepped outside the back door and let it slam behind him. Juana bit her bottom lip while the tears began to stream down her face. She glanced at Tracey on the way through the door.

Tracey did as she was told and went for the broom that was in the small broom closet beside the back door. As she opened its door, she saw Mister going into the barn, pulling his belt off as he walked. Juana reluctantly followed. Tracey knew what would happen next. She felt Juana's fear and remembered the pain the belt left. She vowed then to find the liquid Teodoro wanted. She too would do whatever she had to do to help them escape.

Chapter 11

Matt was on the phone when Maggie came from her bedroom. She had fallen asleep in the chair and hadn't moved all night. Matt leaned against the counter with his elbow resting on the countertop, phone in hand. His other hand held a cup of freshly brewed black coffee.

Maggie went to the cupboards searching for a cup. She found a mug, poured the coffee, then went to the refrigerator looking for cream or milk. She poured a sprinkle of milk, barely turning the color of the coffee.

Matt hung the phone back in its cradle on the wall. "That's odd."

"What's odd?"

"No one at the PD knows anything about the shop owner's story, there's no report, and there isn't anyone working the case."

"No one working Tracey's case?"

"Not now. Sergeant Bradley said Chief Otiga kept all the files at home."

"Isn't that unusual?"

"Not really. Especially in a small department. He probably did a lot of his work at home. But what puzzles me is that he told us there was an officer looking into the eye witness' statement."

"And that's the odd part?"

"Yeah."

"Are you sure Sergeant Bradley knows what he's talking about?"

"He said he's second in command, and since the chief's death, he's been bumped up to Officer in Charge, which means he will be Acting Chief until St. John decides on a new chief."

"How many others are there?"

"The two officers, and one secretary. And with that small of a department, he should know what he's talking about."

Maggie sipped her hot coffee. "What's next?"

"We pay our respects to Mrs. Otiga and see what we can find out."

"Oh, Matt, use the situation to get information?"

"Yep. That's what we PIs do."

Maggie knew Matt was putting her on now. Surely he hadn't turned that cold. Or had he?

"But first, we need to de-Red you." Matt pulled a pair of scissors from the drawer and was squeezing them open and closed.

"You're cutting my hair?"

He grinned at her. "Yep, right again. Don't look so surprised. I've always said a person can do anything…"

"…if they put their mind to it," she finished. "That was a long time ago. You still believe that?"

"More than ever. Now, if you'll follow me to the deck." He opened the sliding screen door and went out first.

She followed him to a chair in the corner. Apprehensively, she sat with mixed feelings, scared and indifferent. She had worn her hair the same way since high school. Her long curly locks reached her shoulder blades, but if cutting and coloring it meant finding Tracey, then she'd do it.

Matt put a towel around her shoulders and started cutting, while humming the song, *Zip-A-Dee-Doo-Dah*.

After a few cuts, Maggie looked out beyond the deck and became mesmerized by the scenery. The hillside leading down to Coral Bay was full of trees and no roads were visible, but the rooftops of houses could be seen scattered about. An ivory beach stretched around the edge of the U-shaped bay and disappeared in the trees directly below her.

The water in the bay was crystal clear and the distance gave the bay different shades of blues, starting with the palest of blue at the beach and gradually getting darker as the water got deeper. It was picture perfect, and for a moment Maggie was sucked into the splendor of the view before her. She felt the warmth of the sun beating down on her neck.

My neck she thought. Maggie touched her neck with her hand.

"I can feel my neck."

"Looks great," Matt confirmed.

She stood and faced him, running her hands through her hair. "How short did you go?"

"Now it's really curly." Matt grinned with pride. He didn't have barbering skills and until now, wasn't sure what he would end up with.

She went to the bathroom and looked in the mirror; her hair was short. In fact, she never remembered her hair ever being that short. Soft flowing curls hung freely around her face to her jaw line, over her ears, and around the back of her head, totally exposing her neck. Matt came in with the hair color box in his hand.

"Step two. Ready?"

Maggie continued to run her hands through her hair. "What color did you say?"

"I didn't, but what we have here is—Natural Blue Black," he read from the box.

She took the box from his hand. "I don't think this is a good thing, but it won't really matter, now will it? I'll do this part myself."

"Whatever you like. I'll just go make a few phone calls."

Matt left the room to make his calls while Maggie read the directions. She had colored a friend's hair one time, but had never done her own. It was going to take twenty-five minutes for the color to set once she applied it, so she got the folder of information Matt had given her and read while she waited.

After the allotted time, Maggie stepped into the shower and came out with a towel wrapped around her body and one around her head. She picked up the folder and went to the bedroom to read a while longer. Matt knocked on her bedroom door.

"Hey, Red. I have to run an errand. I'm expecting a call from my assistant. Just tell him I'll call him back. He might leave some info. Go ahead and write it down."

She got up, went to the door and opened it enough to stick her head out.

"How long will you be gone?"

"Not long." He grabbed the towel from her head. "Hey, not bad!"

"Give that back." She grabbed for the towel, and felt the towel around her body start to loosen and quickly closed the door.

"I'll be back." He laughed.

She went to the mirror and finger fluffed her hair. She wasn't fond of the color, but she had to admit, she liked the cut. Matt told her they would be visiting Janice Otiga today, and she wished she had brought a better outfit for the occasion. The locals dressed casual for every occasion, so her tan shorts and navy blue sleeveless blouse wouldn't be out of place.

The phone rang and Maggie went to answer it. "Hello. Yes, this is Maggie."

"Maggie, this is Pete."

"Pete?" Maggie was stunned to hear the voice from the past. Matt's Uncle Pete had been a New York police officer for forty-one years and had retired two years ago on his sixtieth birthday. Since then, he worked with Matt, helping with the investigation business by doing a great deal of the research. His connections in the justice system gives them unlimited access.

"Your voice sounds wonderful to hear. I've missed you," he said.

Maggie loved Pete. He was a gruff cop, but a kind and gentle man. He always had a story to tell and filled the room with laughter.

"I'm doing everything possible on this end to help you find your daughter, Maggie. How are you holding up?"

"I suppose as well as can be expected. It's the worst thing that's ever happened to me." Maggie swallowed hard to keep down the lump in her throat. Whenever anyone sympathized with her, she had to hold back the tears.

"I called to give my nephew some information, is he there?"

"He went out and said he would call you back when he returns. He didn't tell me you were his assistant."

"You know how he is, full of surprises."

"What are you looking for?"

"Right now, many things. One of the areas I'm concentrating on is getting Tracey on as many missing children reports as possible. She's listed in NCIC, the FBI's National Crime Information Center computer system, and now we have her listed with the National Center for Missing and Exploited Children (NCMEC), who work with Interpol to help find kids outside the states."

"You don't think she's been taken out of the country, do you?"

"Although it's a possibility, we are hoping to locate her in the states. But, listing Tracey with every possible agency gives us that many more people looking for her. Maybe someone from another country was here in the states on a business trip and saw her. They display all the missing children's pictures on Internet web sites, and anyone with a computer will be able to see her picture. The more exposure we have, the better."

Maggie did wonder if someone had taken Tracey to another country, but the thought scared her and she forced it out of her mind. Besides that, her motherly intuition told her Tracey was alive and not too far away. She just had to be right. "I understand."

Maggie heard the rear door of the beach house open and looked around the corner to see Matt struggling to get in the door with a big box he was carrying.

"Pete, could you hold on a minute?" She ran to hold the door for him. He carried the box to the table in front of the sliding doors and set it down, all the while grinning at Maggie's black hair.

"Your uncle is on the phone."

Matt went to the phone. "Pete, what's up?"

Maggie read the outside of the box and listened to Matt's conversation.

"You're in luck. Give me a half-hour to hook up the fax and you can send over what you have. Okay, thanks, Pete. I'll be talking to you soon."

Matt hung up the phone and went to the box. He opened it and pulled out a combination fax/telephone machine.

"Hey, Re…oh, no more red. I'll have to call you by your alias now, Roberta Watkins. You can pack a bag for the beach with your folder while I hook this thing up and do the programming. On our way to the beach we'll pay our respects to the chief's wife."

Maggie headed for her room to slip her suit on under her clothes and pack the beach bag.

"By the way, Bert, I like the black hair. It's very exotic."

Chapter 12

They stopped in front of Janice Otiga's house around 9:00 a.m. There were two cars in the drive, so Matt parked along the road. Maggie dreaded the job ahead and took a deep breath. Even though Tracey was away from Maggie for now, she was sure Tracey was alive, but Janice's husband would never come home again.

"There are probably other people inside with Janice, so remember, we are Roberta and Matt Watkins, vacationers-slash-friends of the chief and his family.

"Janice knows about this?"

"Yes. When I last talked with the chief, he said he'd tell his wife because he knew she'd want to see you."

"I know…we're from New York and you own a restaurant and I do the paperwork for the business."

"I see you've been reading some of the material I gave you."

"The restaurant's called *Matt's,* and you're a rich guy and I'm a rich guy's wife. Let's go and get this over."

Matt got out of the Jeep and walked around to open Maggie's door, but she was already out by the time he got there. They walked to the front door of the modest ranch style home and rang the doorbell. Maggie didn't recognize the woman answering the door.

"Yes, can I help you?"

"I'm Ma…"

Matt cut her off before she could finish.

"We're the Watkins from New York here to see Janice."

Maggie couldn't believe she almost used her real name after the conversation she just had with Matt. She would have to be more careful. She wasn't fond of playing this ridiculous game.

"If you'll wait right here I'll tell her you're here," and she closed the door.

"Wouldn't you think she would have asked us inside to wait?" asked Maggie.

Matt shrugged his shoulders. "Well, she doesn't know us, I guess."

When the door opened again it was Janice Otiga. Her grief-stricken look told the whole story. "Maggie," she whispered, and hugged her. "Please come inside."

Janice Otiga was a beautiful young woman, with long straight brown hair that shone as if the sunlight were on it all the time. She looked more like a runway model than a thirty-year-old mother of two. Janice swore by sunscreen and used it daily, giving her skin a golden brown appearance. Today her face was swollen, and her bright blue eyes were red and puffy from a long night of grieving. She took Maggie by the hand. "Let's go to the kitchen."

The entryway of her home led directly to a small hallway going into the kitchen. Two women stood in the kitchen, the woman who answered the door, and another woman who was doing dishes. Janice took Matt's hand like they'd been pals forever and introduced Matt and Maggie to her friends.

"I'd like you to meet some friends of mine. This is Roberta and Matt Watkins, and this is Carol Wells and Patty Bradley. Patty and Carol's husbands are on the police force. They've been with me all night."

"Where are the children?" asked Maggie.

"They're with their grandparents. Juan's parents didn't want to be alone and they are good company for each other."

Carol finished the dishes and turned to Janice. "Since you have company, I think I will run home and check on my kids, Janice. Then I'll come back at five o'clock to take you to the funeral home."

"I'll go, too, and check on my husband to see if he's eaten. If I don't check, he won't eat," Patty remarked.

Janice thanked them and they left. She sat at the kitchen table and invited Maggie and Matt to sit also. "Can I get you something to drink?"

Maggie declined for the both of them and sat next to Janice. Matt sat next to Maggie at the round table.

"I am so sorry. Is there anything we can do for you? Anything at all?" Maggie asked.

"There's nothing anyone can do now." Janice attempted a smile. "But thanks for asking."

"How are the boys taking this?"

"Chad is only four, so he's a little confused as to where Daddy really is, but Thomas is six and understands he won't be coming home again. We're trying to keep them busy. We have an appointment with the funeral director tonight to make arrangements. After the funeral, I think both boys will feel the effects." Tears dripped from her eyes. "I never knew it was possible to cry this much."

Maggie took Janice's hand in hers and shared Janice's sadness.

Janice changed the subject. "I knew you were undercover, but I had no idea you were changing your looks. I kind of like it, but I bet it looks even better in your natural color." Both women smiled. "Now, tell me what I can do for you."

That was the Janice Maggie had come to know in such a short time. Even in the eyes of her own devastation, she wanted to help someone else.

Matt spoke first. "We need to see your husband's files on Tracey's case. We were told he kept them at home."

Janice shook her head. "He does, but I'm afraid that might take time. You see, last night when I went to the hospital morgue, someone broke into the house and destroyed Juan's office. Let me show you."

Maggie and Matt followed Janice to a small office located in the back of the house. The room was a mess. Everything had been thrown around and left in piles covering the floor. The drawers from Juan's file cabinets had been pulled out and emptied. It looked as though someone had taken the files and thrown them into the air, leaving scattered papers everywhere. The large floor-to-ceiling bookshelves had very few books left on the shelves; the rest were tossed around the room. The small pine desk drawers were turned upside down, with their contents lying on top of the paper ruins. The desktop was wiped clean, with pencils, pens, stapler, clock, telephone, and picture frames, all lying on the floor.

"Have you ever seen such a mess?" asked Janice.

"It's obvious somebody was looking for something," Matt answered. "And this mess was probably left so we can't figure out what that something is."

"That's what Bob Wells said, that's Carol's husband, on the force. Ray Bradley, Patty's husband, thinks it was somebody looking for money. Anyway, whatever the case, I'm afraid it will take a long time to put all this paperwork back in order."

Maggie's disappointment was easy to see.

"Did the police dust for prints?" asked Matt.

"No, they said the burglars probably wore gloves and it would be futile to bother. They wanted to concentrate on finding whoever killed Juan."

Matt could see the broken window in the back of the room. "Is that how they came in?"

"Yes. We don't have an alarm on the house. St. John doesn't have crime, so to speak. At least not like other places. This past year has been the worst in the twenty years I've lived here."

"Where are you from originally?" Maggie asked.

"I'm from Salt Lake City, Utah. My parents moved here when I was ten to open a bed and breakfast. I met Juan in high school and we've been together since." Janice's eyes filled with tears.

Maggie put her arm around Janice's shoulders. "Come on, Janice. We'll go back to the kitchen."

"Do you care if I poke around a bit?" asked Matt.

"Go ahead. Maybe you can find something that the police didn't," Janice said.

The two women left and Matt squatted at the door. He couldn't walk into the room without walking on papers. He picked up a handful of papers directly in front of him and found they were typed pages of a file. The case name was in the top left corner with the case type, and the page number was typed on the top right corner. He searched through several pages, finding an array of names and case types, mostly misdemeanors; Wilson/petty theft, Ross/disorderly conduct, Vega/intoxicated assault. It appeared bar fights and five-finger discounts from local stores were the island's crime problems. *That could explain why the police hadn't searched through this room to see what could be missing,* Matt thought. *They aren't used to handling major cases and the murder is all they can handle at one time.*

Matt walked gingerly across the mounds of debris to get a look at the point of entry. The glass had been shattered by the twist-lock in the middle of the window. Matt was puzzled by what he discovered. The glass bits lay outside the house, indicating that the window had been smashed from the inside. Matt raised the window and stuck his head through the opening. A three-foot area edged with rocks was planted with green bushes and flowering plants. Sand was used as a top coating, with shells, rocks, and driftwood spread around as garden ornaments. None of it appeared disturbed. Matt knew if someone had come in from the outside, he would be able to see a footprint or two in the sand. Instead, the sand was smooth and unmarked, except where the broken glass lay.

Matt looked through the rest of the house on his way back to the kitchen. He saw the Otiga's bedroom next to the chief's office, where a queen-size bed sat against an outside wall. There were windows on both sides of the bed. Only blinds covered the windows, allowing the bright sunlight to come into the room. The windows were open with the trade winds gently blowing through the blinds.

The boys bunked together in one room with a common bathroom between their room and their parents'. The living room was rectangle, with a gas adobe fireplace. Matt wondered if they ever had a chance to use the fireplace in such a tropical climate. The whole house was decorated in a Mexican motif to reflect Juan's heritage. Matt made his way into the kitchen where the women were sipping lemonade.

Janice looked at Matt as he entered the room. "It's a mess, isn't it?"

"That it is. I was hoping you might let me come back tonight while you're at the funeral home and start to clean up."

"You don't need to do that."

"I'd like to say I'd be doing it just to help, but the truth is I'm looking for any paperwork I can find on Tracey's case."

"Of course you are, and of course you can."

"I'd like to keep this between us if we could."

"Yes, anything you need."

More cloak and dagger, Maggie thought.

"Janice, does anyone else have keys to your house?" he asked.

She looked puzzled by his question. "Juan's parents have the only spare. They watch the boys a lot of times and come and go as they please. Why do you ask?"

Matt wasn't ready to reveal to her that whoever ransacked Juan's office didn't come in through the window. Either Janice left the door open when she went to the morgue, or the suspect(s) let themselves in with a key.

"I wanted to make sure when Maggie and I come back tonight no one will surprise us."

Matt made arrangements to return at five o'clock when Janice's friends would be taking her to the funeral home. Janice would leave the door unlocked for him.

Chapter 13

The man known as the Cuban to everyone except his mother, is a rich man and getting richer every day. He owns a huge fortress of a home in Miami, Florida, and surrounds himself with rebels. He had been born and raised in Cuba, but left when he was eighteen and never went back. Because he is an illegal alien living a life of crime, he keeps a low profile, not drawing any unwanted attention.

Over the years, he has handled anything from money laundering to murder, and now employed over two hundred people all over the world to carry out his orders. His latest endeavor has proven to be the most lucrative and the most despicable. His previous endeavors had acquired him the wealth and power he needed to accomplish his present operation. He employs doctors at three of his own hospital clinics located in Zurich, Utah, and Spain, lawyers to handle his business affairs, and pilots to haul cargo.

The Cuban took a cigar from his beautifully handcrafted cherry humidor and swung the humidor around by its lid, pushing it to the far edge of his large mahogany desk. He offered the man sitting across from him a cigar. The man selected a cigar from the box and used the tip-snipper to cut the end of it. He pulled off the gold cigar band and placed it in his pocket. The man reached for the Austrian crystal lighter and lit his cigar, took a puff, and rolled the cigar between his fingers. The man loved smoking the expensive Cuban blend.

"Tell me what this man has done for my organization," the Cuban said.

"In the past ten years he has supplied you with five children."

"And the money he's brought us with those five?"

"Thousands, hundred of thousands. We only need to ask him and he supplies us with the merchandise."

"And where have these children gone?"

"All to Cairo."

"And does this man know where the children are going?"

"No. He thinks they are being adopted."

The man looked at his cigar and continued to play with it.

The Cuban spoke first, breaking the moment of silence.

"And tell me about this Maggie Brown."

"She was on the island three months ago, involving everyone from the local police to the FBI to find her daughter."

"Our man took her daughter?"

"No."

"You say she is coming back?"

"Yes, to meet the chief."

"But we know she will not meet with the chief. I want to know where this child went." The Cuban's thick Spanish accent became stronger when he became angry.

The man began to squirm at the sound of the Cuban's voice. "Maybe someone else took her, or she had an accident of some kind and they haven't found her body yet." He was guessing, of course.

"This is not an operation that has room for error or incompetence. I want you to watch this man closely. See that he is not hiding anything from us. You may leave through the back."

It was a stroke of luck to have overheard Chief Otiga saying that the Brown woman was returning. He was glad he could answer the Cuban's question. So far he hadn't seen her, and if he was lucky, she changed her mind about coming. He stood and touched the top of the humidor with his fingertips. "May I?"

The Cuban nodded.

The man helped himself to four of the imported smokes, placing them into his shirt pocket. He walked across the Persian silk rug that covered the center of the hardwood cherry floor.

The entire room was full with warm rich colors. Two cranberry leather chairs surrounded the six foot by ten foot desk that shone with many layers of varnish. Carvings of lion heads were molded into the edge work on the desk's corners. Carvings of lion feet held the massive piece of furniture up from the floor. The same heads were present in each corner of the room on the cherry crown molding. The wall behind the Cuban's desk was floor to ceiling bookshelves. Rare books, pottery pieces and antique clocks were properly placed on the shelves. He loved collecting antique clocks and fine pottery, and had several buyers to attend city auctions to buy for him. Attending *Sotheby's* auction in New York was one of the rare times he would leave his home.

A fireplace big enough to walk into was along the wall across the room and a six-inch piece of black Italian marble was used as a mantle above the opening. In front of the fireplace sat a navy leather couch and two chintz chairs. The rest of the room was accented in forest green and the deepest gold color available.

The Cuban had three doors in the room, one to an outer office where his secretary sat, a back door that led outside, and a private door that led to the rest of the house. His private bodyguards guarded each door. He always had three men with him wherever he went. He was a direct man and demanded respect from all who surrounded him.

Chapter 14

After visiting with Janice Otiga, Maggie and Matt spent the day on one of the island beaches. St. John has some of the most beautiful beaches in the world that are never overcrowded with people, and today Maggie and Matt were two out of four people on Trunk Bay Beach.

Maggie had plenty of time to read the rest of the material in the folder and ask Matt questions. She caught up on his life, and he with hers. Maggie didn't reveal everything about her past and she suspected Matt left out a few details as well. She managed to find out that there wasn't a woman in his life and hadn't been for many years. He told her he was busy with his business, one thing Maggie attributed to their breakup.

They grabbed a burger at a local diner and parked down the road from the Otiga's house to wait for Janice to leave for the funeral home as planned. They ate their burgers and drank their shakes in the Jeep while they waited. Carol Wells drove by them in an old gray Chevy Cavalier at 4:45. Five minutes later she drove past them again, this time with Janice in the car. Maggie and Matt left the Jeep along the road and walked to the house. The back door had been left open for them.

Looking at the mess on the office floor, Maggie asked, "Where do we begin?"

"Pick up the papers and put them in piles. We'll sort through them when we get them off the floor."

Maggie separated pages from file folders, and found many scrap pieces of paper with notes written on them. She put the notes and the telephone message papers in another pile. She also found many handwritten pages, mostly in the same handwriting, which she assumed was Juan's.

Matt tried to put the desktop back in order the best he could and placed books back onto the bookshelves. He thumbed through the books before he replaced them, thinking he might run across pertinent information stuck within the pages.

Once they had all the papers in piles, they began to put each typed page in piles according to the names on the case files, separating over one hundred cases. The labels had the victim's name and case type written on them. Once she had the pages separated, she and Matt matched the pages with the folder information and began to put the files back in order. They searched for a file with Tracey's name on it, but didn't find anything with her name at all.

"We'll keep looking through the typed pages. Maybe the folder was misplaced." Matt was beginning to think Tracey's file was what was missing.

When they were almost finished, Matt searched through the telephone messages, placing them with their case. Some of the messages weren't marked, making it impossible to guess which case they belonged with.

Matt glanced at his watch at seven o'clock and wondered when Janice would be coming home. He was hoping to be gone by the time she returned.

"Did you find anything with Tracey's name on it?" Maggie asked.

"No, not yet. I'm about to go through the notes he made. I didn't find any phone messages that relate to any kidnapping."

Matt sat on top of the chief's desk separating notes. When he heard a car on the gravel driveway he jumped off the desk and turned out the light in the room.

They waited to see who it was. They heard one car door shut and heard the women say their goodbyes. Janice let herself in the back door with a key. She came directly to the office where Maggie and Matt waited. Matt flipped the light switch on as Janice walked into the room.

"Find anything?" she asked.

"No," answered Maggie. "Were you able to make all the arrangements?"

"Yes. Everyone has been so helpful."

"Are the boys with you?" Maggie asked.

"No. They're staying with their grandparents tonight. Can I help?" Janice looked exhausted.

"We're just about finished," Matt answered.

"The room looks nice—back the way it was." It made Janice sad to see things in order again. It made her feel like Juan would be coming home any minute.

"I'm going to go sit down if you two don't mind."

She left the room and Maggie looked at Matt. "Are we done here?" she whispered.

Matt nodded. He too felt the need to leave Janice alone. He decided to take the rest of the phone messages with him. Before they left, Matt asked Janice for a piece of wood he could nail over the broken window. She said if there was any wood, it would be in Juan's workshop in the back yard.

Maggie sat with Janice while Matt looked for the wood.

Matt saw that Juan had been in the middle of a project. A small toolbox filled to the top with hand tools sat on top of the workbench and a sander was plugged into the electrical outlet. A thin layer of sawdust covered everything. Stackable bins on a shelf underneath the bench held nuts, bolts, nails and other small objects. A half-made wooden box sat in the middle of the bench and another finished wooden box similar to that one sat beside the bins on the shelf. Carved in the top of the box was Juan's first born son's name, Thomas. Matt assumed Juan was in the process of making the other box for his second born, Chad. He found a piece of plywood big enough to cover the bottom of the window, located a hammer and the nails he needed. As Matt was about to pull the string on the light hanging over the workbench, he noticed an open matchbook lying on the workbench below the wall phone. The initials TB written on the inside caught his attention. It was a stretch, but he thought TB could stand for Tracey Brown. He read the other scribblings: *SB FL 462 LA IP, Exp/Imp*. He shoved the matches into his pocket and returned to the house.

It was nine o'clock when Maggie and Matt left Janice. It took them twenty minutes to get to the beach house and, after a full day, Maggie was ready to call it a day and go to bed. She couldn't remember the last time she'd been this tired. Matt on the other hand, wanted to put together the odds and ends he had picked up along the way and to look over the chief's telephone messages.

Juan had been exceptional when it came to note taking, and all but two of the handwritten notes found on his office floor had been placed in the proper files. Even though he used his own shorthand method, the notes were easy to decode. That made the note on the matchbook cover more of a mystery to Matt. It wasn't Juan's usual style to be so brief.

Chapter 15

The Cuban had ordered him to keep an eye on Mister, and at least if he had to spy on someone, he was lucky enough to do it in a tropical climate. He remembered many times watching someone for days in the bitter cold of a Pennsylvania winter. Many times he would be forced to sit in the streets, pretending to be homeless, trying to keep warm by the fire, and watch gang members or some other hoodlums. The pay was as awful then, as were the hours.

The Cuban was a generous man with the people he employed and trusted, and he paid much better. Buying and selling kids was a lucrative business and he was eager to be a part of it, even if it was dangerous. If the Cuban found he couldn't trust an employee, he would make sure they disappeared forever. Mister had been hired on his recommendation to the Cuban, and if he found Mister to be hiding something he would be in trouble too. Mister had been an asset for over twelve years, but he knew people changed, and maybe Mister was losing it.

There were only two gas stations in Cruz Bay and Mister worked at the largest. Harry Burns owned the station and several others on different islands. He had one hired hand at each station to do repairs and one man to pump gas and sell products. Mister had never missed a day of work in fifteen years.

Mister liked his job, but found it hard to make ends meet on his income. That's when he hooked up with the Cuban. At first, he delivered packages for the Cuban around the islands. In six months time he had enough money to buy his own boat and he didn't have to rely on the ferry service to get around. He still took the ferry to and from work and used the boat only for the jobs he did for the Cuban.

Ten years ago he had a meeting at the Cuban's house in Miami. Mister was in awe to see how he lived. The Cuban offered him more money to do a more difficult job. He wanted him to take children. He told Mister he had men working all over the world to handle certain territories, and Mister could handle the islands. He was very familiar with them and the job was easy for him.

Mister and Mama had been married thirteen years and weren't able to have children. This broke her heart. After Mister had taken two children for the Cuban, he realized he could take children for Mama also. She would lie awake nights crying for children and he wanted to make her happy. He didn't tell the Cuban he was doing this. In fact, he felt it wasn't anyone else's business what he did on his own time. Ten years had given Mama nine children and had made her very happy.

Mister heard the ding of the bell as a customer ran over the bell hose at the gasoline pumps. He went out to wait on his customer.

"Can I help you, sir?"

Matt was looking in his wallet, counting his money when Mister spoke to him. "Yeah, fill 'er up, please."

"Yes, sir." Mister went to the pump and placed the nozzle of the hose into the gas tank on Matt's Jeep. He reached for the squeegee and window cleaner. Matt hadn't removed the top from the Jeep this morning and decided to do it now while his tank was filling.

Mister finished cleaning the windshield just as he heard the click on the nozzle. He walked past Matt to take the hose from the Jeep and place it in the holder on the pump.

"Great view of the bay from here," Matt said.

"Yes, sir."

"Awful news about the police chief." Matt tried to engage in conversation.

"Yes, sir."

"Did you know him?"

"Not very well, sir."

Matt could see he was a man of few words. "Worked here long?"

"Yes sir, twelve years. Will there be anything else today?"

"No thanks."

Matt paid for the gasoline and left the station. As he drove, he wondered how someone could work at a gas station for twelve years in a very small place like Cruz Bay and not know the police chief. Matt realized he wasn't a talkative guy, and possibly a little slow, but even Goober knew Sheriff Taylor really well. Matt knew he'd have plenty of opportunities to talk to him again.

The man in the boat watched Mister through his binoculars and rubbed his tongue along his gold tooth in the front of his mouth. That was Mister's seventh customer this morning in one hour, and if that was all Mister did all morning, the Cuban's hired hand knew he would become bored and fall asleep by noon.

Besides, he knew he must make an appearance at work. He decided to abandon his surveillance until Mister got off work at six o'clock that night.

Matt came into town to make a stop at the police station to introduce himself to the department as the chief's friend and nose around to see what they found out about the murder. He pulled into the parking lot of the small building and saw the St. John Police Department sign above the door, with Chief Juan Otiga written below. The flag flew half-mast.

A Jamaican woman in her forties sat at the first desk by the front door. She held the telephone tightly between her ear and shoulder as her fingers moved smoothly over the typewriter keys. She raised her eyes to glance at Matt.

He looked around the room and saw three other desks along the outside walls. There were two windows, one on each side of the room with bars across them. Two steel doors with one small square window in each were at the back of the room. The signs on the doors read: *Holding Area*. Matt wondered if that was the extent of their jail. If anyone had to spend the night, they probably did so in those rooms.

Matt was surprised at the condition of the room. The walls were painted a pastel blue and the ceiling a pastel green. *Very tropical looking*, he thought. Four white ceiling fans swirled to keep air flowing. An open door on the right displayed the CHIEF sign. Matt already knew what he was going to tell them to get a look inside.

"Sorry for de wait. How con I help you, sir?"

"Hi." Matt flashed his handsome grin. "I'm Matt Watkins. I'm here on vacation to visit the Otigas."

As soon as the officer in the room heard what Matt said, he got up from his desk and came to Matt. "Mr. Watkins, I'm Bob Wells. Janice told my wife you were here. What can I do for you?"

"I'm here to see what you've learned about the case and to pick up the chief's things from his office."

The door opened behind Matt and another officer walked inside.

"Ray, this is Matt Watkins, the chief's friend."

"Ray Bradley," he introduced himself as he shook Matt's hand.

"I'm sorry dis had to hoppen while you are here," spoke the secretary. "Did you arrive on de island before de shooting?"

"Yes—did you?" asked Bradley.

"As a matter of fact, I did. I came on the seven o'clock ferry from St. Thomas. Why do you ask?" Matt knew full well why the officer wanted to know. He was wondering if Matt could be a suspect.

"Did you get a chance to see the chief before the accident?" Wells asked.

The accident? So they call murder an accident on St. John, thought Matt.

"And your wife is here too?" asked Bradley.

"Yes, that's right." Matt was hoping to avoid answering Wells' question.

"And how did you say you knew the chief?" asked Bradley.

"My wife and Janice went to school together."

"I must have missed your answer. Did you have the opportunity to see the chief yesterday?" pressed Bradley.

"No, we didn't," Matt lied.

"So what brings you here today?"

"I was hoping to hear you had some leads on the case."

"We are just about to close the case. With the lack of evidence, we are forced to rule this a random drive-by shooting." The sergeant puffed his chest as if he were proud of his decision.

And that's that. It was clear now to Matt that these officers weren't capable of handling a case of this magnitude. "Do you think you'll ever find out who did it?" he asked.

"Probably not. People can come and go as they please here. They can get around by ferry service or by private boat. There isn't a Customs, and that makes it nearly impossible to trace anyone," Wells said.

What the officers didn't know was that Matt held two pieces of evidence that were overlooked by the department. He had gone out before sunrise the morning after the shooting, after the police had been there. He had searched the area and found a tree stump with dried blood and a piece of gray material hanging on it. He could see evidence that something had taken place on the ground, with the sand and leaves scattered about and imprints left. He had also found a novel on the road where he saw the Jeep drive away. The book had the Otiga's address handwritten in pencil on the inside front cover. This indicated to Matt that this was clearly not a random drive-by shooting.

"Janice asked that I box the chief's things and take them to her," Matt said.

"Already done," answered Bradley. "Wells, get that box on my desk for Mr. Watkins."

Matt could see Wells was embarrassed by Bradley's arrogance. Matt left with the box. It was amazing to him to think that while the department was investigating a major crime, they had time to clear the chief's office for the next guy.

Matt drove to the bakery in town to pick up breakfast for Maggie. Before he went inside, he used Maggie's cell phone to call Pete.

"It's Matt. I need you to do some checking for me. See what you can find out on a Patrolman Robert Wells and a Sergeant Raymond Bradley. It shouldn't be too difficult to get their social security numbers. They're with the St. John PD. Also, see if you can run this as a plate. FL462LA—that's Floyd, Lincoln, 462, Lincoln, Adam."

They chatted about the weather and said goodbye. Matt went into the bakery and purchased a half dozen cake donuts and two cups of coffee to go.

Maggie had gotten out of bed when she heard the back door shut as Matt was leaving. The digital display on the alarm clock read 6:00 a.m. She showered and dressed for the day, then waited for Matt to return. She felt like she was stuck in limbo, unable to do anything until she heard from him. The table was full of things Matt had collected so far. She saw the book and piece of material and wondered where they had come from and what they meant. A stack of phone messages lay beside the book and a stack of faxed papers lay beside the phone messages.

Maggie picked up the matchbook cover and examined it. The initials TB jumped out at her, but what did the others mean? She heard Matt come through the back door.

"Bert, I have breakfast."

"What's this?" She held up the matchbook for Matt to see.

"I found it on Juan's workbench."

"Is TB Tracey's initials?"

"They could be related. I'm trying to find out. Does any of that mean anything to you?"

She studied the letters and numbers, trying to make sense of them.

"No, I don't have any idea."

"I'm having Pete run the string of letters and numbers as a license plate. Maybe that's what it is. Are you ready to work today?"

"I thought you'd never ask. What do you have in mind?"

"I'm going back into town to look for the shop owner the chief told us about. I hooked up a computer in my room so we'll have access to the Internet. What I'd like you to do is get on line with the Bureau of Missing and Exploited Children and go back at least ten years to see how many children are missing from the islands, note how they disappeared and what ages they were and check to see if any have been found. The bureau has an e-mail address and can help you do the search. Find any similar cases that sound like Tracey's. You do know how to run a computer, don't you?"

His infectious grin made her smile back at him. "Have you forgotten already that I sent you all the info on Tracey via your e-mail?"

"I thought you had a good secretary or something."

Chapter 16

Mister and the mechanic took a half-hour to close the station, putting oil and antifreeze displays inside and locking the doors. Harry Burns had already stopped to get the end of the day receipts and money from them.

The Cuban's man was hiding in the distance and watched as the men did their work. He had changed from his work clothes and was now wearing baggy shorts, a wrinkled shirt, old deck shoes, and a battered straw hat. The brim of his hat and the sunglasses he wore hid most of his face. He didn't want Mister to know he was following him and tried to stay out of sight by blending in with the surroundings.

He knew Mister took a seven o'clock ferry, but he had never really paid any attention which ferry it was Mister got on. He had his boat ready to go and had a moped on board to follow Mister on land. The Jeep rentals on the islands closed at six o'clock, so he had to provide his own land vehicle. The moped wasn't going to be fast, but would make it possible for him to duck in and out of places quickly.

Mister got into his truck and headed to the far end of the island where the vehicle and cargo ferries serviced most delivery trucks for the island businesses. The Cuban's man started his Jeep and followed Mister to the ferry docks. Mister never left his truck. There were five ferries at this time, each ferry going to different islands. The man was surprised when Mister chose a ferry that boarded only two other vehicles. The other ferries had lines of cars, each hauling to more populated islands.

He waited until the ferry was two miles out, then started his boat. He followed it, staying at least one mile behind. When it was close to land, he went in far enough to be able to see with his binoculars which road Mister was taking. There were only two roads, one going to the right and one to the left. After he saw Mister take the road to the right, he quickly docked his boat. People paid for dockage at the marina, but he couldn't take the time to do that and keep up with Mister, so he brought a sign with him that read, *Official Police Business*, which he hung on his bow rail. He knew no one would question it and would leave the boat alone.

He lifted the moped off the back of his boat and carried it to the street, got on, and started peddling until the motor took over. Top speed was thirty miles per hour and he pushed the bike to its limit to catch up with Mister. Mister was a careful and slow driver, which made it possible for the Cuban's man to find him. Just as on St. John, this island had only the two main roads, so he wasn't worried about Mister taking a turn or two that he didn't see.

After riding a few miles, he caught a glimpse of brake lights. He was sure that it was Mister. The lights turned to the left, but the main road took a sharp turn to the right. There were no houses, no driveways or side roads. He saw dust in the distance on his left and took off in that direction on a hunch that it must be Mister.

The area was nothing but sand and rocks with a few clusters of palm trees scattered here and there. A short way in he saw the taillights on the truck. After driving what seemed like a mile, he spotted an abandoned farmhouse to his right. He saw Mister drive past the empty house. The area was hilly and many times he would lose sight of Mister as he drove over and down a hill. It was also difficult to keep the moped going on such a course. When he started up a hill, the engine would cut off, forcing him to peddle again.

Twilight came, making everything blend together and hard to see. He hoped Mister would turn on his truck lights, making it easier for him to follow, but he never did. Mister disappeared over a hillside, and when the Cuban's man got to the top of the hill he saw a farm sitting at the bottom. The house sat just behind the barn, but from on top of the hill he was able to see the lights from inside the house.

Mister drove his truck into the barn. He walked out of the barn, closed the doors and went inside the house. The man waited for five minutes, left his moped on the top of the hill, and walked to the backside of the barn. He crept around the barn, ran from the barn to the house, and ducked behind a large hibiscus bush outside the kitchen window.

Supper was always ready when Mister got home from work. The children moved around the kitchen in silence, getting the food to the table. Mister washed his hands at the kitchen sink, then sat at the table waiting for everyone else to sit. Mama took her seat at the opposite end of the table and the children sat on the benches along both sides. They bowed their heads, and it was Freiza's turn to say the blessing.

The Cuban's man took the opportunity to peek through the kitchen window during the prayer, hoping no one was looking. What he saw was amazing to him. The man he thought was a bachelor all these years, had a wife and a family. A very large family. When they finished with grace, Mama started passing the food. The Cuban's man found it odd that a family of nine children could eat in silence. The only children he'd ever been around talked all the time.

While they ate, the sun set and the darkness enabled the man to hide behind the bush without fear of being seen. When dinner was over, Mister left the table and went to the living room to sit in his worn recliner and read the daily paper he had brought with him from work. Most of the time he would leave the paper out in the evening after he went to bed and Teodoro would use them to teach the other children to read and write.

The girls began to clear the table and do the dishes under Mama's supervision. Teodoro, Tobias, and Jose started sweeping the floor. Moises took the garbage to the compost pile behind the barn. The Cuban's man peeked though the bush to see where Moises was going. He saw Moises go behind the barn with a large bowl heaped with something inside and minutes later return with the empty bowl.

Mama went to sit in the living room with Mister and picked up her sewing basket full of clothing that needed mending. She picked a pair of boy's pants that needed a patch sewn on the knee. She threaded a needle and occasionally glanced up through her bifocals at Mister. She was checking his mood before she spoke. "The dogs took off after another dog early this evening and haven't come home yet."

He lowered his paper to his lap and looked at her. "That explains why they didn't greet me when I come home. I just figured they was out on the other side of the property playin' with a turtle."

She waited for a moment. "Don't it make you mad?"

"Naw. We don't want no dogs sniffin' around here either."

The Cuban's man began to worry about the dogs, and thought he should head back to his moped before the dogs came back. He would have to check on Mister later when he was prepared to face the dogs. He quickly ran to the back of the barn and looked around to make sure no one was there. The man went up the hill to where he'd left his bike. Just as he reached the top, he heard growling from behind. He didn't need to turn around to know there were two big dogs behind him. Moving forward slowly, he hoped to get on his moped before the dogs decided to come after him.

As he picked up the bike, he heard one dog break into a bark. He swung around just in time to see the other dog lunge at his leg. The dog's sharp teeth sank into his flesh and the man let out a loud scream.

Mister got up when he heard the dog's barking, and heard the scream echo in the distance. He grabbed his flashlight from the kitchen counter and went out the back door to investigate. Mama went to the kitchen door after him, but didn't go any farther. The children gathered around her.

Mister followed the sound of the barking dog and wondered why he could hear only one dog.

The Cuban's man took his handgun from his holster and began hitting the dog on the head. The dog wouldn't let go and the man could see the light from Mister's flashlight jiggling back and forth as Mister ran up the hill. Excruciating pain forced him to fire his gun, discharging a warning. When the dog didn't let go, he shot it. The dog let go instantly and dropped to the ground.

When Mister heard the gunfire, he froze in his steps. The man jumped on the moped and took off. The other dog shied away when he heard the first loud bang from the gun. Mister ran up the hill when he realized the bike sound was going away. He shined his light in the direction of the bike, but it and its rider were too far away to be seen. He reached the top of the hill and found his dog lying with a bullet hole in his right shoulder and a bleeding head wound. The other dog sniffed at his injured partner.

Mister found the strength he needed to pick up the large, wounded animal and start back down the hill toward the farm. When he reached the barn he yelled for the boys. "Mama Send the boys outside."

Mama gently shoved the reluctant boys out the door. "He's calling, it must be all right to go. Now, go ahead."

"Tobias, open the barn doors!" Mister was out of breath. His arms started to shake from the dog's weight.

Frightened, Tobias opened the doors as fast as he could.

"Get the blanket in the back of my truck, Teodoro. Lay it in the horse stall."

Teodoro moved swiftly, eyeing the injured dog.

"There are some old rags in the box by the gas can. Get them."

Jose and Moises looked at each other, unsure of who should get the rags. Moises started wheezing under the pressure. Anytime he was upset, he would experience an asthma attack. Jose went for the rags and Moises felt in his pocket for his inhalator.

Mister laid the dog on the blanket and examined the extent of the dog's injuries. The dog's eyes were open, but he was still. "Get a bucket of water from the house."

Tobias sprang into action. Mister went to his truck and unlocked the glove compartment, taking out a small plastic bottle. He knelt on the floor, took a rag from the box, and unscrewed the lid on the bottle. He poured some of the clear liquid on the rag, then closed the bottle.

Teodoro watched in curiosity as Mister placed the rag over the dog's nose. The dog went to sleep instantly. Teodoro knew the liquid was what he wanted, and now he knew where Mister kept it. He also found out it would work on the dogs.

Tobias returned with the water. Mister took another rag from the box and dunked it in the water. He first washed the dog's head, then washed around the bullet hole.

Teodoro was surprised how gentle Mister was with the dog.

Blood ran down the dog's leg and he washed the area clean. "Dump this bucket and get clean water," he ordered.

This time Jose went.

Mister took out his pocketknife and began probing the dog's shoulder for the bullet. "Teodoro, I need antiseptic and gauze from the house. Ask Mama."

When he walked into the kitchen, Mama and the girls were sitting around the table waiting for more news.

Mama stood. "How is the dog?"

"I'm not sure. He's taking a bullet out of his leg, I think."

"So Jose was right? The dog's been shot?"

"Yes. He sent me in for gauze and antiseptic."

"I'll get them." She left the kitchen to go to the bathroom cupboard.

"What happened?" whispered Tracey.

"One of the dog's been shot. But listen," he whispered and leaned close to Tracey so Mama wouldn't hear. "I know where the liquid is, and I know it works on the dogs. He used it to put the dog to sleep."

"Who shot the dog?" asked Nalda.

"He hasn't said a word about it. He's barking out orders and removing the bullet."

The girls became quiet.

Mama returned with a shoebox. "Everything he needs should be in here." She handed the box to Teodoro.

When Teodoro returned, Mister had removed the bullet and held a rag tightly over the wound.

Mister took the antiseptic from the box and handed it to Jose. "Pour some on a rag."

Jose did as he was told and handed the soaked rag to Mister. Mister cleaned the dog's open wound. He took another clean rag and placed it over the wound. He then took the gauze and wrapped it around the dog's shoulder area, then its body, making a circle around the top of the dog's leg to anchor the gauze.

After several wraps, he ordered Teodoro to cut long strips of first-aid tape with his pocketknife. Teodoro picked up the blood-soaked knife and washed it off in the water. The sticky blood had started to dry and was hard to remove. As ordered, he used the knife to cut several strips of tape for Mister.

Mister told the two younger boys to put everything away and to take the used rags to the burn barrel.

Teodoro and Jose wanted to ask what had happened, but knew better. The questions would have made Mister angry.

"Go back to the house," he ordered.

Teodoro still held the pocketknife in his hand and wondered if he should risk getting caught if he tried to take it with him. He froze for a split second in decision. If he was caught, he knew he'd be beaten and put in the box. When he realized Jose was almost to the barn door he knew he had to move. He held the knife in his closed hand and turned away from Mister to leave.

"Aren't you forgetting something?" asked Mister.

Teodoro stopped and held his breath in fear, and slowly turned toward Mister. Beads of sweat began to run from underneath Teodoro's blond hair. He saw Mister raising the shoebox in one hand.

"Take this back to Mama."

Teodoro took the shoebox from Mister with his empty hand and turned back around to leave. Jose was outside the barn waiting for Teodoro. The two walked together to the house.

The Cuban's man rode the bike all the way to the main road before stopping. His leg was bleeding profusely and he stopped only long enough to check the extent of his injury. He removed his belt and wrapped it around his leg above the knee to stop the bleeding. Afraid Mister was following him, he got back on the moped and headed toward the docks. Luckily, when he arrived at the docks there weren't many people around. Only two men stood at the end of the docks, and they were too busy talking to notice him. The Cuban's man loaded his moped onto his boat and went back to St. John.

Chapter 17

As soon as Maggie heard the door, she got up from the computer to show Matt what she found. "It took me all day, but look at this." She handed him a stack of papers.

"Hi, Bert. Yes, I had a wonderful day, and yours?" he joked.

"Just look." She grinned.

Matt took the papers from her and sat down on the sofa. He put his ball cap beside him and propped his feet up on the coffee table.

Maggie put his cap on the table and sat beside him on the edge of the couch. She pointed to different things on different pages as she spoke. "It seems there have been at least fourteen children, including Tracey, kidnapped or reported missing from the islands close by. This has been during the past ten years, and they are all still missing. There have been others, but they were found—either dead or alive—and some were victims of divorced parents, where one parent took them from the other. Anyway, they've been located."

Matt looked at the information Maggie had given him.

"I've typed a page that lists the missing children in the past ten years to the present. I have their names, addresses, parents' names, social security numbers and their age when they disappeared."

She shuffled through the papers until she located the one she wanted. "I also have individual information about each of the other thirteen cases. Like where they were when they disappeared, if anyone saw anything, and so on. And check this out. All thirteen children disappeared during some sort of festival or parade, just like Tracey."

Matt continued to glance at all the paperwork as Maggie talked.

"Out of those cases, at least eight had reports of eyewitnesses of the children being seen with a clown." Maggie's eyes were wild with excitement. She waited for his response.

"I wonder if the FBI had this information?" he asked.

"If they did, they didn't tell me. Does it help us?"

"It definitely gives us some avenues to explore."

"What did you find out today?" she asked.

"I found our shop owner has taken an unexpected vacation, destination unknown by anyone in town and no return date known. His name is Ivan Price and he owns a hat shop."

"You think he's running from something?'

"Either that or he was asked to leave, or he's disappeared permanently—if you know what I mean."

"Oh, Matt. You think..."

"Well, if someone did do away with him, it was because he knew something that someone didn't want anyone else to know. And that might be good news for us."

"Why?"

"That means someone has something to hide."

"Like Tracey?"

"Maybe."

"How can we find out about Ivan Price?"

"That's why we have Pete."

"Oh." Maggie jumped up from the couch. "Pete faxed some stuff for you." She went to the kitchen counter to retrieve the information. She brought back the papers and handed them to Matt. It was the information he had requested from Pete on the officers at St. John PD.

"It seems Patrolman Robert Wells was born and raised in Chicago and served on the Chicago police department for three years. He married Carol Smith when he was twenty-two years old and took the job on St. John PD six years ago.

"No news there, eh?" she said.

"Raymond Bradley, born in Philadelphia, Pennsylvania. Son of a Common Pleas Judge, he has an expunged juvenile record for assault, petty theft, public intoxication, and he spent one year in a juvenile home for boys."

"If his record's expunged, how'd Pete get all that information?"

"That's my uncle. He can get anything on anybody. You don't have anything to hide, do you?'

She bit her lip. "Very funny. Go on."

"Daddy madc his juvenile record go away and got him into the local police academy. He then worked two years on a voluntary program with a local police department. After that he moved to Kentucky where he worked as a cop full-time. He was married to Amanda Barnett, who already had three kids. He was picked up a few times for drunk and disorderly. It seems Daddy made those records disappear too. After his divorce, he moved to St. John, that's five years ago, to become an officer here. He's not married."

"We met his wife."

"Nope. We met his so-called wife. We'll see if Pete can locate his ex for a few questions and see if he can find out who Patty Bradley really is."

"Why do you care about him?"

"There's something about him I don't like."

"Do you think he knows something about Tracey's case?'

"At this point, we check out everything."

Maggie jotted down what they wanted to have Pete check. She was in the middle of writing the note when she saw something familiar. She went to the table with all the items they had collected and got the matchbook cover.

"Hey Matt, could IP be Ivan Price?"

"Let me see." He got up to take a look at the cover.

"Um…could be. Let's get a list started to what these scribblings could mean and keep it on hand. Maggie got a piece of paper and started the list with TB being Tracey Brown and IP possibly being Ivan Price, shop owner.

"Did you get anything from Pete on these letters and numbers?" she asked.

"He says it's not a plate number and he's checking some other things. Let's make some phone calls to some of the parents of the other thirteen missing kids."

"Are we going to call all the parents?"

"Why?"

"It just seems like we'll be digging up bad memories."

"We probably will, but it might take us a step closer to finding out what happened to Tracey, and possibly help us find out what happened to some of the other children."

While Matt called the parents, Maggie fiddled with the matchbook scribblings, finding possible words to match the letters. She used a dictionary to look up words beginning with TB, SB, FL, LA, IP, Imp and Exp, as printed on the cover.

After five calls, Matt hung up the phone, rubbed his eyes, and looked at his watch. "It's eleven thirty and getting too late to call. Did you come up with anything?' He walked to the table and took a seat beside her.

"There doesn't seem to be any logical word for TB, so we'll just assume for now it's Tracey Brown. SB could be Bachelor of Science, but that probably doesn't have anything to do with our case, so I haven't come up with anything for that yet. Now, listen to this. FL could be Florida, flee, float, flood, flimsy, or flight. If it's flight the numbers could be flight numbers, and if the numbers are flight numbers, LA could be Louisiana or Los Angeles. So we might be looking at Flight 462 to Louisiana or Los Angeles."

Matt took the matchbook cover and looked at the numbers. "You're a genius. And you could be on to something."

"Thanks," she grinned. "As for Exp, maybe it's expose, export, because it has imported right after that, or expensive."

He looked at the words that appeared to run together. "Expose imported?" He shook his head. "Exported imported. Possibly. What did you say the last one was?"

"Expense or expensive."

"Expense imported, expensive imported? Don't know. But for now we'll have Pete look into the flight number. What's IP?"

"Could be Ipecac, a plant grown in South America, or Ivan Price."

"We'll stick with Ivan Price for now. Let's see if Pete can make a flight verification for us. Maybe Ivan Price took that flight."

They wrote down all the information Pete needed. "We'll fax it to him now so he'll have it first thing in the morning when he gets to the office."

"You sure know how to keep Pete busy," she joked.

"Yeah. He's been a great help to me in the business. If I had to do all the work, it would take me twice as long to complete a case." He finished the note and took it to the fax machine to send to Pete. He punched in the telephone number and waited for the paper to go through the machine. He thought about the day's events and his search for the shop owner. He had been all over town, all day long, and no sign of Acting Chief Bradley. The man had rubbed him the wrong way from the beginning. It wasn't something he could explain, it was just a gut reaction, and he didn't like him.

"I'll bet if Pete's able to find the ex-Mrs. Raymond Bradley, we'll get some information from her on our Sergeant Bradley."

"Hey Matt. SB. Could it be..."

"Sergeant Bradley. That's possible. Make a note of it."

Mister went to work as usual, and Teodoro told Mama he needed to do his chores outside and clean the barn. This gave him plenty of time to work on the raft. The injured dog was resting in a pen that Mister had built. He was too injured to be of any threat to Teodoro, or anyone else for that matter. Mister had put the other dog on patrol around the property line before he went to work, which meant Teodoro would be able to move about freely.

Jose came into the barn looking for Teodoro. "Teodoro, where are you?"

"Shhh. I'm up here."

Jose looked up and saw Teodoro peeking his head out from over the loft. "Can I come up?"

"Are you alone?"

"Yes."

Teodoro waved his hand and signaled for Jose to come to the loft. Jose went to the ladder and climbed to join Teodoro. Teodoro was to the farthest back corner of the loft where he was working on his raft.

"Can I help?" Jose asked.

"Yes, but you'll have to be quiet."

"Why? Mama never comes out here."

"Well, you never know when she might need us for something, and she might have to check on the dog."

"The dog doesn't look so good. He let me walk right past him."

"He lifted his head when I came into the barn this morning and has been sleeping ever since."

"Good. He scares me." Jose focused his attention on what Teodoro was doing. "What can I do?"

"Grab one of those boards over there and we'll tie it on next to the rest."

Jose went for a board while Teodoro cut more strips of rawhide that he was using to tie the boards together. In the past he had to sneak Mama's sewing scissors each time he worked on the raft, and then sneak to get them back before she needed them again. Now he had Mister's pocketknife, and could cut whenever he wanted.

"Where'd you get the rawhide?" asked Jose.

"I found it in the pile of supplies in the back of the barn."

Jose watched as Teodoro put the new board in the place where it would be added to the others. "You hold this one and I'll tie them together."

Jose held the board for Teodoro. "How do you know it will stay together?"

"I've tied each board on separately with a different piece of rawhide. When all the boards are in place, I'll lace them together to make sure they won't come apart."

"Where did you get the boards?"

"The loft has two floors and I'm using the top floor. Nobody can see the boards are missing because there's still another row left."

Teodoro pushed aside some of the straw on the floor to show Jose what he was talking about.

"After I get all the boards in place this way, I'm going to make an X with two boards on the bottom of the raft for support too."

"When will you be done?"

"Maybe in a couple of days. It depends how much time I can spend on it."

"Then what will you do?"

"I've already planned how we will escape."

"Who's going?"

Teodoro knew what Jose was getting around to. He was not planning to leave. Jose was too afraid.

"All of us."

"I can't go."

"What do you mean?"

"I can't leave here."

"Don't you want to see your family again? I'm sure they are still looking for you"

"I have many brothers and sisters. They'll do all right without me."

"That's fear talking. I know you want to go home." Teodoro looked at Jose. "You hate Mister and you know Mama isn't much better."

Jose looked at the raft.

"You'll be left here, alone with them."

"I'm afraid. What if we get caught?"

"We won't."

"How can you be so sure?"

The boys became still.

"When I tried to run away I was sure I would make it, too," Jose said.

"That was different. You were alone and didn't know where you were going. But since you ran away before, you were able to tell us what was out there, beyond the farm. Once we make it to the water we'll be able to take the raft to another island where there are people. Then we'll be free."

Jose wanted to believe what Teodoro said. He wanted to run with the others, but he was too afraid of Mister. He was sure Mister would kill him this time if he caught him. When the time came for the children to run he would pretend to have the flu and be too sick to go.

Chapter 18

The Cuban's man would have to wear pants to work to hide the dog bite, or make up a story about how he was bitten. He could tell people he found the stray dog on the beach and when he tried to befriend it the dog became frightened and bit him. Then he would be able to have a doctor look at his leg. He knew if he went to see a doctor he would insist on having the police department look for the dog to do a rabies check. When they weren't able to locate the dog, the doctor would want to give him the rabies vaccination, which was a series of shots in the stomach. The Cuban's man didn't want any part of that. He examined his leg and decided to wait a couple of days to see if it got worse. He knew it was better for him to keep this incident quiet as long as possible.

He was up all night getting the blood out of the carpet on his boat and doing some work on his computer. He had a hunch where Mister had gotten all his children. He noticed the children he saw all looked different, one boy was black and another child looked oriental.

He told his girlfriend about his events during the night and swore her to secrecy, but she was used to it. He had made her aware of his other job, but not all the details. She knew he had another employer and everything he did was not by the hand of the law, but that didn't matter to her. She spent the extra money on fine clothing, jewelry, and lavish vacations. He always warned her not to flaunt her expensive baubles around his co-workers causing them to ask how he could afford such luxuries on his salary.

The Cuban's man had met his girlfriend when she was dancing in a strip club in Miami. He was in Florida to meet with the Cuban and went to the club one night. Maybe it was the booze—maybe he was lonely—he wasn't sure, but he couldn't take his eyes off her. He stayed all night, mesmerized each time she danced. He would stick ten-dollar bills in her g-string when she came near, and after the first ten, she came by his table often.

When her shift was over he asked her to breakfast. She agreed and they never parted after that. She packed her bags and he took her to St. John. They told his co-workers and friends they had been old schoolmates and went to the same vacation spot year after year on vacation and married on the last trip. When she found out how he made his extra money, she kept her mouth shut and lived like a queen, never having to dance again.

The Cuban's man dressed for work and thought about his plans for the day. He would make an appearance at work and spend the rest of the day spying at Mister's house. He wasn't sure if he had killed the dog or not, but he knew he would have to take care of the other dog anyway. He had a tranquilizer gun for wild animals, but he knew that it would be too big to carry on his moped. Instead, he took a hypodermic needle filled with an animal sedative and would use that to disable the dogs for the day. He also knew Mister never missed a day of work, so he wouldn't be around to get in his way.

Chapter 19

It was another beautiful morning on St. John and Matt sipped his coffee and looked out over the bay from the deck.

Maggie watched Matt from the living room. He had his back toward her and was wearing only tan shorts. His legs were propped high on the deck rail as he rested back against the Adirondack chair. His legs and back were a deep brown color from only one day on the beach. Even though Matt and Maggie had only been together again for a couple of days, she felt just as comfortable with him now as she had so many years ago. She was even beginning to understand why he had done some of the things she had questioned before. She knew they had left the chief's side so they could remain in hiding and continue their search for Tracey. After Maggie had watched Matt clean the chief's office and put things back in order, she knew he hadn't just used the situation to gain information.

She poured a cup of coffee and went to the deck to join him. "Good morning," she said.

"And a beautiful morning."

Maggie set her coffee mug on the deck rail so she could pull another Adirondack chair over next to Matt. Once in place, she sat in the chair and crossed one of her legs over the other. Matt watched her from the corner of his eye. Her long, thin legs were slightly reddened by the sun, but mostly white with freckles. They were both aware she was not going to turn the bronze color Matt's skin had become, but that wasn't really Matt's goal in the first place. He only set that pretense in her mind in order to get Maggie to relax for a day. He knew Maggie, and he knew she wouldn't be eating or sleeping while her daughter was missing. He wanted her to have at least one day of rest before they got to work.

"Did you hear from Pete this morning?" she asked.

He looked at his watch, then at Maggie. "It's only eight o'clock, Bert. That's seven o'clock in New York. Pete's probably only been in the office a half-hour. That means he's on his second cup of coffee and third donut."

They laughed, knowing how much Pete loved his sugar.

"Apparently Pete hasn't changed either," she said.

"Either?"

"You're the same too, I think."

"I'll take that as a compliment. I don't think you've changed much either." He paused. "So what happened all those years ago?"

"What do you mean?" Her stomach knotted. She knew all too well what he was asking, and she wasn't prepared to answer his questions.

"To us. If we didn't change, what happened?"

The telephone rang and Maggie jumped to answer. "I'll get it."

Matt was disappointed. For a moment he thought they were about to have the talk they should have had ten years ago. He got up and followed her to the phone.

"Yes, this is she."

"This is John Newman. My wife and I were out when your call came in, but we found your message. You were asking for any information we have on our son Cody, who was kidnapped three years ago from St. Lucia."

"Yes, go on." Maggie motioned for Matt to come to listen. They put their heads together and she held the receiver between them.

"First, I would like to say how sorry we are for your loss and we understand what you are going through."

"I'm sure you do, and thank you."

"Our son was ten when he was kidnapped, just like your daughter. I can send you all the information we gathered at that time. Most of the information we have has already been given to the FBI, but we have our own records as well."

"Was he taken during a festival?"

"Yes, he was."

"Did anyone see anything?"

"Not that we could find. I was taking pictures that day and I have a picture of a clown who I believe is the kidnapper."

"That's great."

Matt pointed to the fax machine.

"Could you fax it to us?"

"Yes, just give me the number and I'll send all the information we have."

They exchanged fax numbers and disconnected. Minutes later a fax rolled through the machine. Matt and Maggie examined the photocopy they held. Maggie felt a rush of adrenaline and became lightheaded as she realized how much the scene in the copy resembled the same scenario that had taken place when Tracey was taken.

The crowd was huddled in a line watching a parade. Mr. Newman had made a circle around his son and a clown in the right hand corner of the photograph. The clown had deflated balloons in his hand and sticking out of a pocket on the side of his jumper.

His face was completely covered in makeup, making big round eyes, large brows, and a huge smile painted in place. In spite of the make-up, it was easy to see his focus was on the little boy. Cody Newman was facing the clown with his back toward his father as he snapped the picture. The boy was bending over trying to pick up a stray balloon lying on the ground.

A beep came from the fax machine and the low humming began as another fax came through. John Newman was sending the other information on his son's case. One page contained a list of FBI officers and their phone numbers, along with the St. Lucia officers and telephone numbers.

"We can call the St. Lucia PD today and see how they handled the case," Matt told Maggie. "I had planned on going to the library, schools, and doctors today with Tracey's picture to see if anyone has seen her. We can take the picture of Cody and the clown with us too."

"The police and FBI already asked around about Tracey."

"Yeah, that's true, but we'll do it again. Something new could have developed. I'm making dinner reservations at *Bon Appétite* for tonight. We *are* supposed to be fishing for a chef, you know?"

"If we ask around about Tracey, won't they be suspicious?"

"Maybe. We'll just say we know the mother as a regular customer and when she heard we were coming, she asked us to check again to see if anyone has seen her. I'll send this picture of Cody to Pete and have him check with the other missing kids' parents. Maybe they have similar photos.

Chapter 20

This trip, the Cuban's man didn't dock at the marina on Culebra Island. He went just north of there to a tiny deserted beach, where he knew he could drive his boat all the way in and anchor on the beach. This time he was ready for the dogs. He used his moped again to get to Mister's house.

Culebra Island is seven miles long and three miles wide, with a population of approximately 2,500, a little more than half of St. John. He checked his maps and found this particular part of the island was the least inhabited. Mister had isolated himself and his family from everything and everyone, being only fifteen miles from St. John, making it easy daily access.

The man left his moped in a clump of trees on top of the hill above Mister's house. He used his binoculars to get a closer look. He didn't see any people outside, but did see one dog rustling through the compost pile. He thought he might have killed the other dog the night before and watched for awhile until he decided it was time to call the dog. A silent dog whistle got the dog's attention. The Doberman lifted his head from the trash and looked in his direction.

The Cuban's man placed a raw steak on the ground two yards in front of him. The dog was downwind, and when he caught a whiff of the meat, his laid-back ears perked slightly. He made a move and the dog came running. When the dog was halfway up the hill, it slowed its pace, growled, and bared his teeth. His focus began to change the closer he stepped to the steak.

The Cuban's man slowly began to extend the metal pole he held in his hands. A leather muzzle hung from the end of the pole. Dogcatchers and other animal trainers used such a pole to trap animals. With the pole fully extended, he moved forward slowly, approaching the dog, who was already licking the meat between growls. With one swift move, the man lunged forward and hooked the dog with the muzzle. The dog began to squirm backward, trying to get free. The man held onto the pole as the dog thrust himself back and forth. The hypodermic needle was between the man's teeth. He used one hand to hold the pole and the other hand to take the needle from his mouth. He popped the plastic needle cover off with this thumb, then readied the needle steady in his hand. He retracted the pole with one quick movement, which allowed him to be close enough to administer the shot.

The dog pulled backward with all his strength, but it was too late and the sedative took over. His breathing became labored and his movements slowed. His legs crumpled beneath his body and he staggered to the ground. The man removed the muzzle. The dog's mouth opened instantly and his tongue rolled out the side of his mouth. He panted until he passed out.

"Sleep, big beast, sleep," murmured the man.

He gathered his equipment and stuffed it into the bag he had strapped onto his moped. Before putting the binoculars away, he took one last look around the property. Still, he saw no one. He wiped his sweaty face off with his handkerchief and shoved it back into his pocket. Just like the night before, he went down the hillside to position himself behind the barn. He waited there a few minutes to catch his breath. He heard voices coming from inside the barn, but they were too low for him to make out any conversation. He found a crack in the barn siding where he could peek and see inside. He could hear the sound of rustling straw and see dust and pieces of straw coming from the loft area, but he was unable to see any people. In the middle of the barn sat the caged dog, covered with bandages. The man knew then he had not killed it.

He decided to make a run for the bush beside the house to take cover. He crouched low to the ground and crept along the outside of the barn, constantly checking for people. As he ran across the open area between the barn and the house, he could see people moving about in the kitchen through the open screen door. He dove for the bush at the corner of the house.

"Evita, would you get the bucket and mop for me while I finish sweeping the floor?" Tracey asked.

Tracey swept the floor debris onto the back porch through the open door, then from the porch to the ground. She had already shaken the rag rugs and they were hanging on the porch railing. Mama made the children wash the floor every day after breakfast and dinner.

Evita got the bucket from the closet and had to reach above her head to place it on the kitchen counter. She opened the cupboard beneath and took out the bottle of cleaning agent. Evita was too short to reach the faucet on her own, so she pushed a kitchen chair in front of the sink. She set the bucket in the sink, unscrewed the cap and poured some of the cleaner into the bucket. She then turned on the water and started filling the bucket.

"Lenora, I have the water running," she called to Tracey.

That was Tracey's cue from her little friend that Evita wanted her to check the water temperature and finish the job. Tracey closed the screen door behind her as she went back inside. Nalda and Freiza came to the edge of the kitchen from the living room and stopped. Each of the girls was carrying a clothes basket with clean, wet clothes inside.

"Is it all right to come through?" Nalda asked.

"Yes, I haven't started to mop yet," answered Tracey.

The two girls walked through the kitchen on their way outside to hang the clothes to dry. Evita jumped off the chair and her dress flew up around her waist.

"Can I come too?"

"Sure. You can hold the clothespins for us," answered Frezia.

"You should wear your sandals," called Tracey. But she was too late. Barefooted Evita was already outside.

The man in the bushes had been peeking in the window and was forced to crouch to the ground when the girls came outside. The clothesline was on the other side of the house and the girls walked the other way. Still hidden by the bush, he looked around the corner to see where the girls were going and to see what they looked like, making a mental note of their approximate ages. He heard voices from the barn and saw Teodoro and Jose walking and talking their way through the doors. The man quickly ducked his head back into the bush. The boys got to the back porch and stopped because they could see Tracey mopping.

"Hey, Leonora. Could we get some water please?" yelled Jose.

It was another hot morning and the barn loft had no moving air, which made the boys hot and thirsty. Tracey stopped mopping, filled two glasses with water and brought them to the boys.

"How are things coming along?" she asked.

"Pretty good. I think I can be done sooner than expected," answered Teodoro. "We need to talk to all the others and make definite plans."

"I don't see how we can get everyone together without looking suspicious."

"You and I will make the plans, then when I'm alone with the boys in our room I'll tell them, and you can tell the girls when you're in your room."

She nodded as the boys handed their water glasses back to her. The man in the bushes wondered what the kids were planning. The boys went back to the barn and Tracey finished the mopping.

The Cuban's man took the opportunity to sneak back to his moped where he had left his supplies and his camera. He had taken a camera from work because he knew it was better than his own. It had a telescoping lens and he would be able to get close-ups from high on the hill. He took pictures of the three girls hanging clothes and snapped one of Tracey when she came to the back porch for the kitchen rugs. The Cuban would want the entire story, so he took pictures of the house and its surroundings also.

The man had suspicions that the information he found on the missing kids from the Internet was going to coincide with what he saw at Mister's house. *Mister must have kidnapped children for himself.* In this entire world, the man could not imagine why someone would want that many kids around. He stayed until late in the afternoon and took more pictures. He saw two other boys come outside one time and took their pictures as well. He took shelter from the sun in the trees and used the opportunity to enjoy one of the Cuban's expensive cigars. He took a drag from it, then ran his tongue across his gold tooth and gently blew the smoke from his mouth.

Keeping an eye on the time, he started putting things away to leave. His girlfriend had made plans to meet with friends at a bar that evening and he needed to get back home. Besides, his leg was starting to ache and he wanted to prop it up a while before they went out.

Chapter 21

"I still can't believe no one around here knows anything or saw anything," Maggie said to Matt as they walked to the beach house.

"We aren't finished looking for today." Matt reminded her. "We still have people to talk to at the restaurant, then maybe we'll check out a few night spots."

"As I recall, there are only two night spots—as you call them," she joked.

"Yeah, you're right." He grinned. "Those are the two we'll check out tonight."

He looked at the time. "Just enough time to take a quick shower and get dressed, but I'll check the fax first. See if..."

When he looked up from his watch, he saw Maggie was already reading a fax.

"What do you have, Bert?"

"A fax from Pete. It says Ivan Price *did* go to Los Angeles on Flight 462."

"Hey, you're getting good at this. Now we need to find out why he left so suddenly—or do you know that too?"

Maggie continued to read to Matt from the fax. "He's already doing that. Pete says he has some buddies on the LAPD and they're looking for Price. When they find him, they're going to pull him in for questioning."

"Does it say when Price took that flight?"

"Yes. The day before we got here."

"That's the same day he told the chief what he saw."

"That's too much of a coincidence."

"You sure are catching on quickly." Matt took the fax from her and read directly from the paper. "The ex-Mrs. Bradley died in a mysterious car accident. She and Bradley had an argument and she took the kids to her mother's, then checked into a motel. The motel manager said he saw her with a guy he thought was Ray Bradley, and the two of them were outside her motel room arguing. She left in her car and he in his. She drove the car off the road and into a ravine—she died instantly."

"Do they think Bradley was involved?"

"He didn't have an alibi and was questioned by police, but there wasn't enough evidence to charge him. Pete talked with Bradley's ex-mother-in-law, who now has custody of the kids. She's convinced Ray Bradley murdered her daughter."

"Does Pete say anything else?"

"Just that he'll keep in touch."

Pete left a message at the bottom of the paper in very fine print that read "I hope you two are getting along nicely." Matt didn't bother Maggie with Pete's humor. He checked his watch again.

"We'd better get moving if we're going to keep our reservation."

They showered, dressed and arrived at the restaurant with five minutes to spare. Matt was wearing navy slacks, a white polo shirt and a tan sportcoat. His cologne was the same he had used the night of their class reunion. Maggie remembered the soft masculine scent.

He held out his arm for her to take. "Mrs. Watkins, shall we go inside?"

Maggie took his arm and played along. "But of course, Mr. Watkins."

They walked up the long entry ramp that was covered with dark green indoor/outdoor carpeting. The same color canvas awning hung above. Matt pulled on the large brass handle to open one side of the arched doors. Stained glass wall sconces illuminated the foyer. A very tall, very attractive blond in her twenties stood at the podium.

"Good evening. May I help you?"

"Yes, we have a reservation for Watkins," Matt told her.

She checked off the name on her list, picked up two leather-covered menus and said, "Right this way, please."

Matt gave Maggie the lead. She wondered if Matt was watching the girl in front of her. She was wearing a white satin slip dress that zipped at her waist and laced the rest of the way up her back in a criss-cross design. Maggie wished she had brought better clothing, feeling out of place in her floral sarong skirt and teal silk tee. She wasn't aware that Matt was only looking at her. They were seated at a table by the window overlooking acres of tree-covered rolling hills.

"Is this part of the Virgin Islands National Park?" she asked.

"Yes, it is," answered the hostess, as she handed them the menus. "Enjoy your dinners."

"That's one reason this island is such a quiet place to visit. Most of it is protected by the park and can't be built up like some of the other islands. And that was a big concern when Tracey and I picked this place. We were tired of all the noise and rushing around."

Matt looked around the room. The restaurant was just starting to fill with people. "I see some people I know."

"What?" Maggie turned her head to see where he was looking.

"It's the Smiths. The people I told you I rode with in the taxi."

He got up from his seat. "I'm going over to say hello."

The Smiths were sitting two tables away, also by the window.

"Hello. Enjoying your stay?" Matt asked.

Mrs. Smith was reading a book and Mr. Smith was reading the daily newspaper.

"Why, it's Mr. Watkins. How nice to see you. Mr. Smith, do you remember Mr. Watkins?"

"Of course I do. Mrs. Smith thinks I forget things."

"Are you here to look for a chef?" she asked.

"Yes. How did you like your dinners?" The Smith's plates were empty, coffee cups half full.

"Wonderful as always," she answered.

"I see you're reading, eh? May I?" Matt took the book from her hands.

"Of course. I just love this author. I've read every one of her books. She always goes into such great detail in her mysteries."

"Joan Garnet," he read aloud. "I don't believe I've read any of her books. And I see you're catching up on the news of the day, Mr. Smith. Is that the St. John paper?" Matt handed the book back to Mrs. Smith.

"No. It's the paper from St. Thomas."

"Well, it was nice to see you again, but I must go now. I haven't ordered yet," explained Matt.

Mrs. Smith stopped him from leaving. "Mr. Watkins, we never got the name of your restaurant, and once in a while we take trips to New York City. I would love to eat there the next time we make it to the city."

Matt patted his jacket pockets, as if he were looking for something. "I usually carry business cards, but I'm afraid I didn't bring any along this evening."

"That's no problem. Mr. Smith, hand me your pocket pen. Mr. Smith always carries a pen."

He gave her the pen and she opened the cover of her book. "I always write notes to myself in my books, and I always have a book with me. Now, what's the name?"

"Matt's."

"Isn't that your first name?" Mr. Smith asked.

"Yes, it is." Matt answered.

"And the restaurant's address?" she asked.

"It's on the corner of West 28th and 8th Avenue, near Chelsea Park on the upper west side. If you do come to my restaurant, be sure and ask for me. I'll give you my best table. Now, I really must run."

Mr. Smith attempted to stand to shake Matt's hand. His bad leg buckled, causing him to fall gently back into his seat.

Matt grabbed his arm to steady him. "Are you all right Mr. Smith?"

"Yes, yes I'm fine. A bit of gout or something."

Matt noticed the bandages around Mr. Smith's calf.

"Looks like you've injured yourself."

"My leg gave out and I tripped on a staircase."

"You'd better have that gout taken care of," Matt said.

"I'll do that Mr. Watkins. Thank you."

"By the way. Where are you staying?" Matt inquired. "Maybe I'll drop by and give you a menu from my restaurant. I have some back at the beach house."

Mrs. Smith was delighted by the idea. "We're at the Palms Motel on Northshore Road, just past town. It's a small, but comfortable and affordable place to stay." She laughed. "We're in Unit 3. Do drop by."

Matt returned to Maggie. They ordered, ate and asked waiters, bus boys, and cooks a lot of questions about Tracey and the restaurant business. They weren't able to find out anything new on Tracey, but they learned a lot about the restaurant business.

"Which hot-spot are we going to first?" asked Maggie as they drove out of the parking lot.

"We're going to make another stop first."

"Where?"

"I have a feeling."

"About what?"

"About the Smiths. It's kind of like a woman's intuition."

"That's a bold thing to admit," she joked.

"Yeah, I'm a heck of a guy. Listen, this might be nothing, but remember the book I found when the chief was shot?

"Yes."

"When I was talking with the Smiths tonight, Mrs. Smith was reading another book by the same author and she said she's read all her books."

"So?"

"She asked the name of my restaurant and didn't hesitate to write it in the front of her book. She said she always did that. The book I found on the side of the road where the chief was murdered had his address written in pencil inside the front cover, and it was the same author. I can't be sure, but the handwriting looked similar. Then when Mr. Smith tried to stand, he fell back into his seat. He claimed it was gout, but he also had an injury that was wrapped with bandages. I think he could have fallen that night and hurt his leg on the stump where I found dried blood and the piece of material."

"You think he's the murderer?"

Matt shrugged his shoulders.

"He's an old man. Well, not old, but a murderer?"

Matt shrugged his shoulders again.

"And you're saying Mrs. Smith is part of it too?"

"I'm only saying we should check it out."

"Where are we going?"

"To their motel. They're staying at the Palms Motel."

"We've driven by there many times. It's just up the road here."

She couldn't believe that such a nice looking couple could take part in a murder. She thought Matt was really reaching for anything. He drove past the motel slowly, turned and stopped. There were ten units at the L-shaped motel, with Unit 3 being close to the office. The office area was built like a house and sat closer to the road than the rental units. All the windows of the office were to the front, making it easier for Matt and Maggie to access the unit without being seen.

He parked the Jeep at the end of the motel, on the side of the last unit with the Jeep facing the road in case they had to leave quickly. It was dark outside and the lighted sign in the front flashed, *NO VACANCY*. Maggie saw there were only two Jeeps in the parking lot and thought that most of the guests must be out for the evening. Maggie and Matt got out of the Jeep and walked toward Unit 3. He took Maggie's hand in his as they walked across the front of the motel to the Smith's room.

"We'll knock on their door first to see if they're there. If they are, I'll tell them I wanted to introduce you to them. If they aren't there, we'll be free to look around," Matt said.

"You mean break in?"

"I like to refer to it as letting myself inside." He grinned.

Maggie could feel her pulse rate accelerating. "I never broken the law before. Well, there was this one time when I was fourteen or fifteen years old.

I was with a group of girls at a mall and a jewelry store had a basket with a bunch of plastic bangle bracelets inside of it. All the girls took one and I really didn't want to, but I caved into the peer pressure and…"

"Shhh." Matt could tell Maggie was anxious by her nervous chatter. "Are you going to be able to do this, or do you want to wait for me in the Jeep?'

She jerked her hand from his. "I beg your pardon. Anything you can do, I can do."

"Anything?" he joked.

"Oh, you know what I mean."

He took her hand again. "Now let's pretend to be a couple, sweetie."

Maggie was nervous. She was praying they wouldn't get caught by the manager, the police, or worse—the Smiths, especially if they were involved with the chief's murder.

"Did you bring a gun?" she asked bluntly.

Matt was amused by her question. "As a matter of fact, yes. But I also brought a stungun, and that's really a lot of fun. I'll show you how it works later."

She loved his sense of humor in a tense situation, but she wasn't sure by his answer if he really did have a gun or not. Although she hated guns, she wanted him to have one tonight.

Matt knocked twice on the door, and when no one answered, he pulled a small leather case from the inside pocket on his sportcoat. The case contained several small metal tools. He selected one and inserted it inside the keyhole on the Smith's door.

"Do you have to go to school to learn how to pick locks?" she asked.

"I see your sense of humor has returned."

"Did it go away?"

They were inside in a second and Maggie felt less vulnerable. The drapes were drawn shut, so they wouldn't have to worry about anyone seeing inside. Matt flipped on the light. The room had two double beds, a round table at the window, a large dresser, a wet bar with an apartment size refrigerator, and a walk-in closet on the back wall by the bathroom.

"You go through the drawers and I'll check around the room."

"What am I looking for?"

"Anything that might link them to the murder."

She opened a small dresser drawer and found a stack of men's underwear. She stared at them, leery of going through someone else's things. Matt saw her hesitation, and came to her.

"Let me show you how to do this." He ran his hand underneath the underwear, touching the bottom of the drawer with the palm of his hand. "Just run your hand through and feel for anything but clothing. In the deeper drawers, you can look around the clothing also."

Maggie nodded and opened the next drawer. She ran her hand along the bottom and on the sides of Mrs. Smith's underwear. The next drawer had men's shorts and undershirts inside. She continued searching. Matt walked around the room looking in the night stand drawer, under the beds, making his way to the closet.

"Matt, look at this." Maggie was holding a large over-stuffed manila envelope in her hands. She went to the bed and dumped its contents.

Matt picked up a stack of one hundred-dollar bills and thumbed through it. "There must be forty or fifty hundreds here," he said.

"And at least twenty stacks. Why would they carry around this kind of cash?"

"Maybe they're loaded and this is spare change."

They looked at each other and shrugged their shoulders.

"Let's put it back and keep looking," he said.

Maggie put the money back and opened the next drawer. Matt went to the closet and started searching through a box he found on the floor. It contained snorkeling equipment, two masks and two pairs of flippers.

"I found their return flight tickets, Matt."

Matt left the closet and went to look at the tickets Maggie held.

"Two tickets, round trip from Denver…Denver?" he questioned.

"What's wrong?" she asked.

"I believe the Smiths said they were from St. Louis." He handed the tickets back to Maggie. "Put them back and keep looking."

Maggie found she enjoyed searching through the room, especially since she had found two things that seemed important to Matt. She and Matt heard the car doors outside the motel room at the same time. Maggie froze in her spot while Matt leaped over both beds to get to the light switch.

"Get down " he whispered. He flipped off the switch instantly, darkening the room. He heard laughter and footsteps coming from the people outside.

"Are they coming here?" Maggie whispered excitedly.

Matt withdrew his gun, a Browning BDA .38 Super Auto from his sportcoat pocket. He backed up against the wall between the door and the window and held the drape open with his finger to look outside. A man, a woman and two teenagers were walking past Unit 3. Matt took the opportunity to look around the lot to see if anyone else was there.

Maggie could hardly breathe. Matt stood in the light from the flashing sign, holding his gun upright, ready to use. It was certainly like a scene from a movie. She remembered when they were together and he was a New York cop. He dressed in his blue uniform every day and strapped on his gun belt, but she had never seen him ready to use his gun. It was an impressive sight to her, but frightening as well.

He flipped the light on and looked at his watch. "It's not the Smiths, just other vacationers, but we'd better get moving. They could be back any minute."

She got up from the floor quickly and went right back to work. She was anxious to get done and out of the room.

Matt went back to finish his search in the closet. He ran his hand along the closet shelf, underneath the spare blanket and bed pillows. His fingers came within inches of the Remington rifle that the Smiths had used to kill the chief. Maggie kept hearing noises which made her more anxious to get the job done and get on their way. She went to the front window to peek outside. Matt reached above his head to pull the pillows from the shelf. He shook them, feeling for anything that might be inside.

"You'd better be careful doing that," he told her. "If the Smiths do pull in, they might see you."

"Oh, I barely opened the curtain on the edge. I don't think…" She turned to look at Matt. "Matt, look " She pointed to the shelf.

He backed up and stood on his tiptoes, which allowed him to see the rifle lying on the shelf in the back.

"Well, what have we here?"

He stood on the bed to see it better. Looking around the room, he located a tissue box and got off the bed to get one. He pulled one of the chairs at the table to the closet door and stood on it. He wrapped the tissue around the barrel of the gun to pull it close to him. If there were fingerprints on it, he didn't want to wipe them off, or add his.

"Could it be the gun that killed the chief?" Maggie asked.

"It's a .22 caliber. The newspaper said that's what killed him," he said. "Now let's put everything back and get going." Matt put the gun back in place and the pillows in front of it. As he stepped off the chair he noticed a pair of men's pants hanging over a hanger in the closet that were the same color as the piece of material he had found near the stump in the woods. He held the pant legs up and found the torn area. "This about cinches it, Bert."

"What's that?"

"Torn pants. He's got an injured leg and I've got the piece of material left behind from his pants."

They both heard the Jeep pull in at the same time and snapped their heads around to the front window. Through the small gap in the middle of the drapes they could see that the headlights were directly in front of the unit.

"Get the light and follow me," he told her.

Panicked, Maggie ran for the light switch. Matt rushed to close the closet door and returned the chair to the table. Maggie was by Matt's side instantly, latching onto his arm. They went to the bathroom to search for a way out and located a sliding window in the shower area. Matt had to stand in the bathtub in order to reach high enough to open it. Only half the window opened, making the opening about two feet wide and one and half feet high.

"Come on," he whispered.

Maggie stepped into the tub as Matt used his fist to punch the screen to the outside of the window.

"You go first," he said.

"It's not big enough."

"It has to be big enough, it's all we have."

He gave her a step up by lacing his fingers together. She stepped up with one foot and grabbed the window with her hands. She went headfirst through the small opening, stopping her fall with her hands. Matt could hear Mr. Smith inserting the key into the lock. With one jump, he bolted through the window. His shoulders were almost too big to get through. The sleeve of his coat dragged the sides of the window, ripping one at the shoulder seam. He fell to the ground, landing on his shoulder. Maggie helped him stand and they ran to the end of the motel toward the Jeep.

"Don't look back, just keep running," said Matt.

They jumped into the Jeep and drove away.

Maggie was trying to catch her breath. "Boy, that was close." She smiled with relief. "I didn't think we were going to fit through that window."

"The cell phone's under your seat. Call the St. John PD, but don't tell them who you are. Tell them you know who killed the Chief and give them Smith's address. Tell them there's a gun inside, and lots of money, then hang up."

Maggie did exactly what Matt said. "What will the police do?"

"They'll go to the Smiths with a search warrant, find the evidence, and arrest them."

"Why would they want to kill Juan?"

"I believe them to be hit men, and the real questions is, who hired them to kill Juan, and why?"

Chapter 22

The raggae band's smooth sound seemed especially sweet to the Cuban's man this evening. He was drinking his second gin and tonic and puffing on a cigar. His girlfriend usually made him dance, but she knew the condition of his leg and she was forced to converse with her friends all evening. He wasn't fond of dancing and was enjoying the relaxation. His girlfriend was sitting at the bar with two women when he felt the vibration from his pager.

"Damn," he sputtered. He assumed at this time of night that it had to be the Cuban. He probably wanted the information on Mister. No one else he knew ever paged him after nine o'clock. He went to the bartender and asked to use the phone behind the bar. He pulled out his pager and pushed the button to light up the digital display. The number was not the Cuban's, and he was surprised to see what number it was. He dialed the number and she answered on the first ring.

"Okay. I'll take a look." He pushed the off switch on the cordless and handed it back to the bartender. He told his girlfriend to stay put, he would be back soon and left the bar.

Chapter 23

Matt took a right turn on the road that led to Hawkness Bay Beach. "We'll sit here for awhile, then drive back past the Smith's motel to see what's happening." Matt told Maggie.

One of the island's wild donkeys strolled past, stopping briefly to check to see if they were handing out food. When it learned they weren't, it vanished in the woods. The soft sandy road was short, leading right to the water's edge. They could smell the salty ocean and feel the gentle night breeze through the trees that surrounded them. A waning crescent moon shined brightly above, casting shadows from the trees.

"Will there be enough evidence to hold the Smiths?" she asked.

"I'm sure of it. All they really need to do is match the gun with the bullet and the Smiths to the gun."

"I'm beginning to think Ivan Price is a prime suspect, and that this is all about Tracey's abduction," Maggie said.

"And you're starting to think like a cop," he joked.

"No, really. Listen." She used her finger to count. "One, the chief talks to Ivan Price about what he saw. Two, Price leaves town quickly and quietly. And three, Smiths—the hired guns—show up here and kill the chief. Why? I think it's because he was getting too close to the truth." Maggie waited for a reply from Matt.

He thought for a minute, then said, "I think you're on to something, but if Price had something to hide, why would he tell the chief what he saw?"

"I don't know."

"Maybe our real suspect paid Price to leave, then had the chief killed."

"Why wouldn't they kill Price too?"

"Good question. Maybe they didn't think it was necessary. If that's all Price saw, he wouldn't be any further threat."

"Have we waited long enough? I'd like to see what's going on," Maggie asked.

They pulled onto the road and headed back toward the Smiths' motel. Matt was impressed with Maggie's skill of deduction. But then he knew she was a very intelligent woman. Even under the stress of hunting for Tracey, she was calm enough to think logically.

"Tell me about Tracey," he said.

Her mind was on the task at hand and his question puzzled her. Why was he asking about Tracey now?

"What exactly do you want to know?"

"What's she like? Is she smart? Is she athletic, what?"

"Yes, she's smart. She's always gotten good grades. She loves people...and has lots of friends. She's just getting to the age where her friends phone her. It's funny, because they don't really chat yet, so they make noises in the phone and say, 'how did that sound on your end?'"

Matt laughed as Maggie continued. "She likes art. I suppose that's because she's been raised around it, and she's very knowledgeable about it. She can tell the difference between impressionist and expressionists, and knows what to look for to spot reproduction sculptures. Tracey spends a lot of time with me at the gallery when she's not in school, so she's savvy to the lingo. She is full of life—and fun—and always looking for fun. She's an optimistic person and finds the good in everyone."

Matt could feel Maggie's excitement as she talked about Tracey.

"She's a self motivator and no job is too big for such a small person. She always says, 'you can do anything...'"

"If you put your mind to it." Matt laughed. "Smart girl."

They smiled at each other, knowing that was Matt's favorite saying. He rounded the bend in the road and could see the motel.

Maggie expected to see lots of flashing lights and people standing around.

Instead, everything looked quiet. Matt slowed to get a good look.

"There's the chief's car. See it?" she asked. The florescent Chief of Police sign on the side of the Jeep was easy to see in the dark.

"Bradley must be inside. I wonder if Wells is with him?" Matt continued past the motel. "Are you up for stopping at a bar?"

"Sure."

"We'll go to the one where I've been told most of the locals go. It's outside of town and tourists don't always find it."

It was another fifteen-minute drive from where they were, and during that time Maggie continued to tell Matt about Tracey. Maggie told him her favorite color, the foods she liked and disliked, and that she was very good at softball. She told him about Tracey's stamp collection and that she started collecting because she and Maggie traveled often, and stamps were something small and affordable to collect. Maggie knew many business associates from all over the world and had asked them to send Tracey stamps. Before their conversation was over, she made Matt agree to send stamps when he could. Matt was happy to agree, but he wanted to *find* Tracey first. Maggie talked as though Tracey would be back in her arms any day now. Matt wasn't that sure.

"We're here," he announced. Matt left his torn coat in the Jeep and put his gun in his pant's pocket.

The bar sat in the middle of a field, with two houses sitting a hundred feet behind it. The bar had been a small service station at one time and it was easy to see the covered-up windows and garage door. The main building was red brick and the openings had been patched in with green aluminum siding. It looked as though the original station sign remained on the roadside, only now it said, Corky's, instead of Shell or Texaco. The building was surrounded by cars.

"If all these vehicles have more than one person in them, then it must be standing room only inside," she said. "How'd you find out about this place?"

"Remember the blond hostess?" He looked at her to see her reaction. "She told me to come by if I wasn't busy tonight."

"Yeah, right." Maggie smarted.

"When we get inside, try to engage people in conversation, then work in your questions. Otherwise it will sound like you're pumping for information."

She nodded, and they went inside. Maggie was right. People were standing everywhere, but she knew it would make it easy to mingle and talk with people this way. If everyone were sitting at tables, she would have to find a reason for approaching them. This way she could saunter up next to someone and start talking.

The two of them made their way to the bar. The room was dark, noisy and hot. Only ceiling fans swirled to create a breeze. Matt asked for a draft and Maggie ordered a soft drink. She didn't want any alcohol and wanted to keep a clear head.

Matt went one way and she the other. The band played and several people danced on the small area in front of the band. Maggie liked raggae music, but had never danced to it. Before she had time to pick out someone to talk with, a man grabbed her drink out of her hand, set it down on a nearby table, and twirled her onto the dance floor. His large stature was intimidating, but his warm smile let Maggie know she was safe. Everyone on the dance floor was smiling and having a good time.

They danced the duration of the song, then the man thanked her for the dance and left her on the dance floor. Maggie went for her drink and made her way back through the crowd. Everyone either clapped or patted her on the back like she had won an award of some kind.

Patty Bradley was coming toward Maggie, waving her hand in the air. "Roberta, Roberta Watkins."

Maggie waved back and walked toward her.

"Hey, nice to see ya." Patty's slurred words proved she had had too much to drink. "Come on over to our table." She grabbed Maggie's wrist, causing Maggie to spill her drink.

Patty dragged Maggie through the crowd to a small cocktail table where she and her friends were sitting. Two women and one man waved as the two of them neared the table.

The man got up and took an empty chair from another table, placing it beside his chair. "Who's your friend?" he asked.

"This is Roberta, everyone. Roberta, this is everyone." They all laughed at Patty's introduction.

"Hi, I'm Mike." He stood to shake Maggie's hand. "This is Sue," he pointed to the woman with short, bleached blond hair, "and this is Corky, the owner of the joint."

"I see you have a nearly empty glass." Corky said. "I'll get you another, on the house. What'll it be?"

"I'm drinking soda."

"Soda ," Patty said excitedly. "No one at this table drinks soda and gets away with it. Make it a hi-ball, Cork." Again, everyone laughed with Patty.

"We see you met the local hoofer right away," said Mike.

"Who?" asked Maggie.

"Dario Raz. Born and raised on St. John. He is the sixth generation of his family to live on the island." Sue continued, "And it's quite an honor to get a dance with him. He'll only dance with women who can keep up."

"How would he have any idea if I could keep up?"

Corky returned with Maggie's drink and set it in front of Maggie, who had taken a seat beside Mike.

"He's been dancing here many years. He has an eye for picking people." Mike winked at Maggie.

Patty sat beside Maggie and took a long gulp of her drink, leaving it only a quarter of the way full. The band played a slower song.

"I wish Ray was here," whined Patty.

"Where is he?" Maggie asked the question, but knew he was at the Smith's.

"He had to go on a call." Patty pouted.

"He wasn't dancing anyway, Patty," Mike said.

"Thats right." Patty's words slurred together and were almost inaudible. She sat with her forearms resting flat on the table and her head was bobbing, causing her to jerk intermittently, resisting the urge to pass out. "He hurt his leg"

"How?" Maggie asked.

"Hespitten…" her voice trailed off.

Corky and Mike nodded to each other and then stood, each taking one of Patty's arms, forcing her to stand.

"We'll take her to the bed in the back," Corky told Mike. "She can sleep awhile until Ray gets back."

Maggie watched as they escorted her past the bar and down a hallway. Looking at Sue, she said, "No one seems to notice."

"She does this often. If things don't go her way she drinks too much, and tonight she was unhappy because Ray wouldn't dance with her."

"How did she say he hurt his leg?"

"I don't really know. He didn't tell us he even hurt his leg. We just thought he didn't wanna dance."

"Are you from around here?" Maggie asked her.

"Yep. Live in the back."

"Are you married?" Maggie had to raise her voice a bit to be heard over the band.

"No. I like the single life. I'm a cashier by day and a barfly by night." Sue laughed. "How about you?"

"I'm here on vacation with my husband. We are friends of the Otigas."

"Oh, sad thing. Juan was such a nice guy and everybody misses him."

"Yes, I know. Have the police come up with an idea of who could have done such a terrible thing?"

"No. Patty says Ray thinks somebody came over from another island and was maybe drunk or somethin', and shot him. Just like a regular person, not because he was the chief."

"Is that what you think?"

"No," Sue paused. "In fact, most people think he was targeted. But nobody has a clue why." She slid to the chair beside Maggie and brought her drink with her. Maggie could smell the heavy scent of alcohol on her breath. Sue leaned in close to Maggie. "Most of us don't think much of Ray as a cop, let alone the new Police Chief. He's a know-it-all and doesn't work much. We don't know why the chief kept him around, except that the chief was such a nice guy he probably felt sorry from him."

"What about Patty?"

"Patty's had a hard life." Sue looked around to see if anyone else could hear. "She was fifteen when she was kicked out of her house. Her alcoholic mom had a new husband and thought Patty was makin' a move for him. She ended up on the streets and became a stripper. That's how she met Ray. They tell everybody they went to school together, but they really met in a club in Miami. Patty told me one day a long time ago—when she had too much to drink. I guess he felt sorry for her."

"It seems like St. John has had its fair share of crime in the past few months."

"What do you mean?" Sue asked.

"There's Juan's murder, and a few months ago a friend of ours was here on vacation and her ten year old daughter was kidnapped."

"Oh yeah. I remember. It was during the Fourth of July parade."

"Yes. Do you know anything about it?"

"Only what I read in the paper."

"I thought since you were such good friends with Patty, maybe she told you more."

"No. Patty said Ray was really quiet about it and never told her about that case."

Maggie took a sip of the drink Corky had given her and choked. She wasn't sure if it was because of its alcohol content or the fact that she looked on the dance floor and saw Matt dancing with the blond hostess from the restaurant. *It was true. She must have told him to come by. What kind of information could he be fishing for on the dance floor?* Maggie excused herself from Sue's company and told her she was going to dance. She looked around the bar to locate her tall, dark, island friend that she danced with before.

"Excuse me, Mr. Raz, could I bother you for another dance?"

"Ya, dat would be my pleasure, miss."

There were more people on the dance floor than the first time she danced, but the crowd seemed to move out of Dario Raz's way and give him extra floor space. Maggie could see the respect the locals gave him.

Matt saw Maggie and waved to her. She lifted her hand and yelled, "Hi, husband," for the benefit of his dancing partner. Matt could see what Maggie was up to and it amused him. At the end of the song, the band announced they were taking a ten minute break. Everyone left the dance floor for their drinks. Matt slithered through and around people to catch up with Maggie.

"Bert, how's it going?"

"Just fine, and you?" she coolly responded.

Matt didn't bother to answer her question. "Weren't you sitting with Bradley's better half?"

"As a matter of fact, yes. But she passed out and the owner and a friend hauled her to a back room to sleep until Bradley comes back."

"Bradley won't be returning for a while."

"I found out from her friend that Bradley isn't liked too much on the island and she said Patty was a stripper when they met."

"Interesting." He thought for a moment while rubbing his chin. "Since Patty's passed out and Bradley's busy, let's go check out their place."

He took her by the hand and led her through the crowd to the door.

"You leavin' already?" It was Mike.

"Yes. We want to get an early start in the morning," answered Maggie. "Maybe I'll see you again."

Matt pulled gently on her arm and they left. "You make friends fast. Let's see, that's two women and two men in such a short time."

"Yes, and it seems you only met one blond all evening." She was proud of herself for responding so quickly to his sarcasm.

"Somebody has to keep an eye on you to make sure you're safe."

"Oh, please. I've been on my own a long time, keeping myself and my daughter safe." Maggie lowered her head and took a deep breath.

"That's right." Matt said quickly. He opened the Jeep door on the driver's side. "Why don't you drive?" he said, wanting to take her mind off their conversation.

"I guess," she sighed. "It's been awhile." She jumped in and Matt handed her the keys.

"You point the way."

Dario Raz was outside, leaning with his back against the building. He watched them drive away.

Chapter 24

Mr. and Mrs. Smith packed as fast as they could under Chief Bradley's supervision. It was obvious somebody was on to them.

"Make sure you take this with you." Mr. Smith handed the .22 rifle to Bradley. "It's your fault that this has happened. If you would have taken the gun away as you were told to do after the shooting, this would not have happened." Mr. Smith's easy-going nature turned hostile.

"Who do you suppose could have come here and found out about us?" asked Mrs. Smith.

Ray Bradley knew he should have come for the gun as the Cuban had directed, but he found himself too busy to bother. He thought it wouldn't make any difference, now he found it did matter. Because of his negligence, he had to reveal himself to the Smiths.

"It doesn't matter now. You'll be gone tonight. I'll take your things in my car. You drive your Jeep to the rental building and leave it there with the keys in it. Walk to the library and I'll pick you up in the back where it's dark, and we'll go to my boat from there. I've made arrangements for you to stay in Red Hook on St. Thomas. Don't move until you hear from me."

Chapter 25

"We're going in on foot," Matt explained. "Park on the next block up and we'll walk back. Bradley's house looks dark, so I don't think there's anyone home."

Maggie pulled to the side of the road and they got out and walked back. The Bradley's owned a ranch house similar to the Otigas', but in a larger neighborhood. Maggie and Matt passed one house with a couple sitting outside on the front porch. They nodded and said hello as they passed.

"We'll go to the back door," Matt told Maggie.

The back of the house had a cement patio covered with an aluminum awning. A glass topped table sat in the center of the patio, surrounded with gothic style metal chairs that had puffy stripped-turquoise seat cushions. Sliding doors led into the house. Only the screen door covered the opening. Matt went to the door and opened it.

"Must be a trustworthy neighborhood," Matt said as he stepped inside.

The house was dark except for a small table lamp that sat on the corner of a telephone stand. Matt used his flashlight to look around the room. A gaudy lime green, fluorescent green, and sky blue floral sectional couch took up one side of the room. The other side had a fifty-two inch screen television with a stereo unit. Multi-shaded gold shag carpeting covered the floor.

"Should I look in another room?" Maggie asked.

"You look here for now until I check out the rest of the house to make sure there aren't any surprises."

She started with the mass of papers, magazines and books that covered the coffee table in front of the sectional, while Matt roamed the rest of the house.

"Bert, in here."

Maggie made her way to Matt who was in a small bedroom. Once inside, she saw the desk, file cabinet and computer.

"You start looking through the stack of papers on the desk and try not to change anything. We don't want them to know someone was here. By now, Bradley and the Smiths must know someone was in their motel room. They must have seen that the screen has been pushed out in the bathroom."

Holding his small flashlight in his mouth, Matt rifled through the file cabinet. Maggie held her flashlight with one hand and searched with the other. She glanced at a paper that looked familiar to her.

"Matt, here's the same information from the Internet on the missing kids that we have."

Matt stopped what he was doing to look at the computer printout.

"Do you suppose he was doing research on Tracey's case?" she asked.

Matt didn't answer, instead handed the papers back to her. "Keep looking."

She took the papers from him and put them back, making sure they were in the same place as before, then continued leafing through the stack. She found a St. John PD Policy and Procedures manual and many other papers pertaining to the department. Below that she found a packet from a travel agency.

"Looks like somebody's taking a trip." she said.

"Why do you say that?"

"There are brochures to Paris, England, Alaska and other places."

"Those are expensive trips." Matt commented.

Maggie looked at Matt. "What are you holding?"

"Bradley has files on all the personnel at the police department."

"Shouldn't those be at the station?" she asked.

"You'd think so. He also has files on four FBI agents."

"Let me see." Maggie went to the cabinet to take a look. She took the files from Matt and laid them open on the desktop, one at a time.

"I know these men."

"You know them?"

"Yes, these are the FBI agents that handled Tracey's case. He must have been working on Tracey's case also, especially since he has the information on the missing kids and now this."

"But he's the one that told me only the chief was working on it."

Matt put the FBI files back into the cabinet and kept going. He knew they were running out of time. It was late and the bars would be closing soon. Even if Bradley wasn't done with his investigation of the Smiths, someone would probably be bringing Patty home soon.

"Bingo." Matt was holding a file in his hand and a smile on his face. He scanned the pages. "Just as I thought. The chief suspected Bradley of doing something wrong too. He's made notes in here to check on him."

"What are you looking at?" Maggie asked.

"The chief's file on Tracey."

"What? Let me see." Maggie was so taken aback by what Matt said that when she wheeled herself around sharply, she hit the stack of papers she'd been going through and the papers fell to the floor.

"So much for keeping things in order." Matt laughed.

Maggie squatted down to pick up the papers, trying desperately to keep them in order. "That proves it," she said.

"Proves what?"

"Bradley must have been working on Tracey's case...or, did he take it from Otigas' house?"

"My precise question also."

Matt was entertaining the idea of taking the file with them when Maggie spoke up. "Hey, Matt. There's a copy machine behind you. You could copy the file and take the copies with us."

"So there is. You must have been reading my mind." He turned the small tabletop unit on and picked pertinent information to copy.

Maggie was picking up the last pieces of paper when she noticed a shoebox on the floor under the desk. She pulled the topless box out to look through it. It was full of pictures.

"What's that?" he asked her.

"Just some pictures of a farmhouse."

"From what I can see in Tracey's file, the chief was working on her case every waking hour. There are many entries with dates and times that shows he was doing everything possible to find her."

"I told you he was. Not just because he was a good chief, but because he had taken a personal interest in us, in fact..." Maggie stopped talking because of the lump that was forming in her throat.

"Yes?" Matt said when she didn't continue, "I'm listening." Matt turned to see her.

Tears streamed down her face. She tried to wipe them away so she could see the image in the photo. He squatted beside her, and when he saw that she was holding a picture of Tracey, he put his arm around her. It was a dated photograph, with the date appearing in the lower right corner.

"Today's date," Matt said softly.

Maggie put her arms around Matt's neck and cried. "She's alive, she's alive."

He held her in his arms for a minute and wanted to stay that way longer, but knew they had to keep moving.

"And Bradley knows where." He stood, taking the box of photos with him. "We'll make copies of these also."

Maggie pulled herself together with a renewed inner strength. Her daughter was alive, and she was going to find her. Matt finished making the copies and made sure things were put back in place, then they left. Matt drove this time.

"When I was snooping around, I found several pieces of expensive jewelry in their bedroom, and a closet full of designer clothing and shoes. And they have expensive electronic gadgets."

"Like what?"

"You saw the state-of-the-art stereo and the wide screen TV, and the computer is the top of the line with all the perks. They've either hit the lottery, or they have a money tree somewhere we didn't see."

"Do you think Patty's still a stripper?"

"She couldn't make that kind of money stripping in the islands. He has a closet full of guns and ammo. He also has a laundry room with enough fishing equipment to supply a charter boat, and it's the best you can buy. He has a large pottery bowl on his dresser that's full of these." He pulled a small gold ring from his pocket and flicked it to her. She caught it and examined it.

"A cigar band?"

"Not just any cigar band. That's one of the most expensive Cuban brands, and one that is illegal in the states."

"How do you know that?"

He smiled. "I read a lot. There's something not right about this whole thing."

Maggie tried to guess what he meant. "If he knows where Tracey is, why doesn't he tell someone?"

"Yeah. Something like that. Tomorrow morning I'll tail Bradley, see what he does during the day."

"What will I do?'

"You'll have to stay by the phone and wait to hear from Pete."

Matt had to think of a quick answer. It was much too dangerous for Maggie to go with him to follow Bradley. Matt knew he'd be able to move faster alone, and if Bradley did lead him to Tracey, he wasn't sure what kind of danger would be involved trying to free her.

Chapter 26

Tracey and Teodoro met in the bathroom. They knew they were taking a terrible risk, but it was necessary in order for them to escape the next night. Everyone had been in bed for an hour, but only Mama and Mister were sleeping. All the others knew about the rendezvous and were waiting for them to return.

Mister snored loudly, which made it easy for the children to be sure he was sleeping. Mama, on the other hand, didn't make any noise and they were guessing she had fallen asleep by now.

"Tomorrow night we go."

"Tomorrow! I thought you said a couple of days?"

"We got done today. Now listen. We'll wait until Mama and Mister have been in bed awhile to make sure they're sleeping, then we go." Teodoro told Tracey. "I'll go first to put the dog to sleep."

"Do you have the liquid?"

"Not yet. I'll get it tomorrow after supper. I'll take the trash out and do it then."

"How will you get into the glove compartment?"

"I'll use Mister's pocket knife. If I can't open it, I'll break into it somehow. It won't matter if I mess it up because we'll be gone when he finds it. Tomorrow is meatloaf night and I'll slide some of my meatloaf off into my napkin. After Mama and Mister are asleep, I'll sneak out of my bedroom window. When the dog comes, I'll lay a rag soaked with the liquid on the ground with the meatloaf on it. The dog will eat the meatloaf, and hopefully, the smell of the liquid will be enough to make him sleep. Then I'll put the rag over his nose and leave it there so he won't wake up until we're gone."

"When will we leave?"

"Right after that. I'll get the boys and we'll go to the barn to get the raft. I'll send Moises to your window to get you and the other girls. You must tell them to be very quiet. Not to make any noise, or speak at all until I tell them it's all right. Do you understand?"

"Yes." Tracey could feel herself shaking with the thought of escaping, but she sure wanted to go home.

"Do you have any questions, Leonora?"

She thought for a moment then said, "No. But after we leave I want you to call me Tracey from then on."

He took her hands in his, smiled and nodded his head. "Yes, I understand."

They left the room separately. Without making a sound, they went back to their rooms to inform the others of their plans. Only little Evita was able to sleep during the night, not fully understanding what was happening.

Chapter 27

When Ray Bradley had gone back to Corky's and found that Patty was sleeping, he took a seat at the bar to have a couple of drinks before going home. Sue walked to the bar and stood beside Ray.

"I just checked on Patty and she's still out. If you need help getting her to the car, let me know."

"Yeah, thanks," He swivelled around on his stool and put his arm around Sue's waist. "That's my Susie. Always ready to help Ray."

She backed away. "Come on, Ray."

"What's the matter?"

"I don't think you should be doin' that."

"Doin' what?" He threw his hands into the air. "Just sayin' thanks to an old friend?"

Sue wanted to change the subject. "The chief's friends were in tonight."

"Who?" Ray turned around on the barstool and continued to drink his beer, acting like he didn't care.

"Roberta Watkins."

"Watkins?" He held the glass to his lips. "Was she alone?"

"What do you mean?'

"Was her husband with her?" Sue could hear the annoyance in his voice.

"Don't know. Patty brought her to our table, but she was alone then."

"What'd she have to say?"

"Nothin' much. She was concerned about Patty. She mentioned the chief's murder, and then she was askin' about that girl that disappeared last July."

"Girl?"

"Yeah. She said the girl is her friend's daughter." Because of his irritated state, Sue hesitantly asked, "Do you know where they're from?"

"No," Ray said sharply. He was irritated that she had been asking questions. He finished his beer, set the glass on the bar, and twisted off the stool. "Gotta go." He went to the back room to check Patty's condition. She was sleeping, huddled in a fetal position. He thought it would be best to drive his vehicle to the back and carry her out the rear door. Carrying his drunken wife out the front door wasn't the kind of attention a new chief wanted.

He checked the clock on the dashboard as he turned the corner onto his street. It was 1:35 a.m., and he was extremely tired since he hadn't gotten any sleep the night before. He passed Matt and Maggie going the opposite direction.

"The Watkins?" Ray said under his breath. "What are they doing in my neighborhood?" He thought it odd because St. John had only two main roads and everyone traveled them to get to the beaches, shopping centers, hiking trails, and restaurants. Most visitors were apprehensive to travel the side roads because of their poor condition. They were primitive at best, and people weren't eager to explore them in their rentals. The rental companies gave maps of primitive roads that were explorable, which detoured the locals around the private residential areas.

Ray turned his car around to follow the Watkins. Ray knew Patty would be asleep all night and not remember anything about that evening. There was something suspicious about the Watkins, and he thought it was strange that the chief had never mentioned them.

It was hard to follow someone on St. John's winding and hilly roads and he needed to stay close to the Watkins or he would miss if they turned into a driveway. He was worried that they might notice him. Ray wished he had Patty's car instead of the chief's marked vehicle.

Matt pulled into the driveway of the Bayview. Ray knew there was nothing he could do tonight, but he would be back in the morning to investigate the Watkins.

It was raining and Maggie and Matt ran from the Jeep to the beach house. It had rained every night since their arrival around the same time of the early morning hours. The rain lasted long enough to keep the foliage green and lush.

Maggie poured a glass of Merlot and went out onto the screened porch. The wind was blowing gently and felt good against her face as she stood next to the screen sipping her drink. Matt looked for a fax or message from Pete. There wasn't any, so he poured a glass of wine and joined Maggie on the porch. He found her sitting on the glider and sat beside her. He lit the three wick candle on the table in front of him using the matches he had gotten from the kitchen. He pulled the gold band from his pocket and played a game of toss with one hand.

"How does a person buy illegal cigars in the United States?" Maggie asked.

"Just like anything else illegal, from someone on the street. But getting something from a communistic country is riskier. They are very expensive and smuggling them into the states adds to their value, and the price to buy them goes even higher, making one very expensive imported item."

"What did you say?" she asked, but didn't wait for him to answer. "You said expensive imported. That's the other group of letters on the matchbook cover." She went inside to get the cover. "Look, Imp/Exp." She handed it to Matt.

"You're probably right. And after seeing the reference to Sergeant Bradley that the chief put in Tracey's file, I'm sure he knows something he's not telling anyone. The chief must have been questioning the cigars. Maybe that will lead us to who Bradley is working for."

"What makes you think Bradley's working for someone?"

"It's the money. He's not making enough at the police department to buy the things they have."

Maggie unfolded the copy of Tracey's picture she held in her hand. She hadn't let go of it since they left Bradley's house. She tried to see Tracey's face clearly, wondering if she looked healthy.

"Where could she be, Matt? Who has her, and why? We know she wasn't taken for ransom, or I would have been contacted by someone, so...why?"

Matt took the picture and held it up in the light from inside the house.

"This doesn't tell us much, except one very important thing. That Tracey is very much alive." He grinned and put his arm around her.

"Yes, but how do we find her?"

"We start with Bradley. I'll tail him, and you can fax all of this to Pete in the morning. Then when you call him, tell him everything we found out tonight. Send him the copies of Tracey's file and the pictures of where Tracey's being held."

Matt continued to look at Tracey's picture. He had already looked at photos of her that Maggie had given to him, but this one looked very much like a young Maggie.

"She looks a lot like you in this picture."

Maggie smiled. "Yes, but that's when I had red hair."

Matt knew Maggie was joking. "Well, this is a black and white copy, so she looks exactly like you." His joking lightened the mood.

Maggie took a drink of her Merlot and sighed deeply afterward. She knew it was going to be hard to fall asleep tonight. The air smelled of wet earth from the rain. Two of the island's small lizards were keeping them company, one on the floor beside the screen, and one on the ceiling on its way inside. She was used to the tiny creatures being about.

"Maggie?"

She thought his tone of voice had changed from carefree to solemn, and he never called her Maggie unless he was serious. "Yes?" she questioned.

"When were you married, and are you divorced?"

Maggie had been trying to avoid this conversation with Matt. She didn't have any way out this time. Trying to keep the subject light she said, "I thought you were the detective."

"No, really."

She could see there was no use trying to avoid his questions any longer. "I never was married," she answered.

"Oh," Matt was somewhat surprised. "I'm sorry."

"Don't be sorry. It's what I chose."

"And Tracey's father?"

"What about him?"

"Do you see him often?"

"No."

"Does Tracey see him often?"

"No." She squirmed in her seat. Talking about Tracey's father always made her uncomfortable.

Matt could see her hesitance. "He doesn't know about her, does he?"

"No," she spouted defensively. "I was pregnant after we went our separate ways. I knew he really didn't want to get married and never wanted children."

Maggie looked at Matt. She could see it bothered him. "I thought it was best," she said.

"What did you tell Tracey?"

"I've always been honest with Tracey. I've told her the truth from the beginning. And she knows it was my choice to do it this way."

"Doesn't she want to know her dad?"

Maggie stared at the flame on the candle. She had dreaded this day, but knew it would come. Until now, no one asked questions about Tracey or her father. Maggie was an only child, and her parents had died in a car accident when she was twenty-three. If her friends brought up the subject, she would find a way to change it. It wasn't hard to keep things from others, especially when she had a good reason.

"She's only ten and just now starting to ask questions and demanding answers. I was using our July vacation as a way for us to have some quality time, and then I was planning to have the two of them meet." She took Tracey's picture out of Matt's hand and looked at Tracey. "I even showed her an old snapshot of him, but he was younger then, and he's changed a little."

"Then you have seen him recently?"

She nodded her head.

"How did you plan to break the news to him? You know, when you thought it was time for them to meet?"

Maggie detected a note of bitterness in Matt's voice. "You see This is why I haven't bothered. You're questioning me like I've made this drastic mistake."

"Hey, Bert. Not so defensive. I was just trying to find out the facts. I didn't mean to hit a nerve. But if it were me, I would want to know. That's all."

"Well, it's not for you to decide, and I'll tell him when I'm ready." She got up abruptly and went into the living room.

He went after her. "I know you love Tracey more than anything and have only done what you think is best," he explained.

Maggie heard the sincerity in Matt's voice. She looked into his eyes and a thousand flashbacks ran through her mind. She remembered how much they had loved each other, how much she had loved him, and knew she still did.

Matt took her arm and drew her close, stopping only long enough to see the love in Maggie's eyes. He leaned in to kiss her, but she pulled back quickly. Their conversation had made her feel sick inside, as though she had made a complete mess of her life. Matt was someone she had always respected, and he was telling her that she had done the wrong thing about the most important thing in her life.

"I always thought I was such a good mother. But I've lost my daughter and now you're telling me I've made a huge mistake raising her altogether." Maggie finally gave in to her feelings, all of the different emotions she had suppressed for months surfaced. When she left Matt, she vowed never to need anyone again and spent the following years trying to convince herself, and others, that she was strong, confident and independent. In one moment, one conversation with Matt, the wall she had been building for years came tumbling down around her.

"No, Maggie, I'm not. I'm saying I would have done it differently. And from what you tell me, Tracey is a wonderful girl without any kind of emotional scarring at all. You've been honest with her, and that's what matters. You need to remember that even though she is your only family, you do have people who love you and want to be a part of your life. My Uncle

Pete, for example, loves you as much today as he did ten years ago. And so do my parents. They have never stopped asking about you.

"I've asked myself many times over the years what I did. What did I do to make you leave me? Why did you run from me, and how could I have stopped you? The night of our class reunion I thought you had come back to me, only to find out you'd left the next day, again. Maggie, didn't you know then that I still loved you?"

Maggie slumped to the couch and didn't answer him. She started crying uncontrollably.

Matt sat next to her, put his arms around her and stayed with her until she was asleep.

Chapter 28

The Cuban's man was on hold, waiting for the Cuban to answer his call. He had never called the Cuban before sunrise, until now. He was afraid of how angry his call would make his boss, but he knew it was imperative to call as soon as possible and tell him about Mister, the children, and the Smiths. He would have to approach the subject of the Smiths with extreme caution. The Cuban didn't tolerate anyone who disobeyed a direct order.

"Sí, what is it?" he answered.

The man could tell the Cuban was not thrilled by his call. "I am sorry to bother you at this time of day, but I have a full day ahead of me and I don't know when I'll get to a telephone again," he started.

"Just tell me what it is you want," demanded the Cuban.

"I followed Mister to his house on Culebra Island. He has a wife and nine children. However, the children are not his biological children. I believe he has been abducting children from around the islands for himself."

The Cuban broke in quickly. "For himself What kind of nonsense is this? The man must be an idiot."

"He has the Brown girl, who was taken three months ago from St. John. I have taken pictures and have all the information on the missing kids for you. I'll send them this morning."

"Sí. And you stay by a telephone until you hear from me, understand?"

"Yes." As irritated as his boss was now, the man decided not to tell him about the Smiths. He would wait until the Cuban called him back. As soon as he disconnected, his phone rang.

"Hello."

Mister spoke quietly. "There's some guy nosin' around town about the chief's shooting and a missing girl. He's askin' a lot of questions about Price and says he's a friend of the chief's."

Watkins, he thought. "Do you know if he's with someone?"

"He's been alone every time I seen him. He was just here a few minutes ago gettin' gas and he was alone then. You gotta do somethin' about him."

Cuban's man was losing his patience. "Hey, don't tell me what I have to do. I've done some checking on my own, and I've found out you've been holding back on me."

"Wha…what?"

"Don't play stupid with me. Where'd you get those kids at your house?"

His question took Mister by surprise.

"You know I had to tell the Cuban about this."

"You told him!" he yelled.

"Yes, and I know you have the Brown girl."

Mister was starting to sweat. *How could he know?* Then he realized. "It was you. You shot my dog. You were at my house that night."

"You shouldn't have hidden this from me, and you shouldn't have taken kids for yourself."

"It's better that I got them than what you do with them."

"You don't seem to mind on payday." Bradley thought they had talked enough. "For now, this is what you do. Keep your mouth shut and keep a low profile. Understand?" The Cuban's man hung up.

Mister placed the phone back in its cradle and looked up. The mechanic was staring at him from the garage area. "Everyting all right?"

"Yeah." Mister saw there were two customers at the pumps. He wiped his head off with the bottom of his shirt and went to wait on his customers.

Matt had washed his own windshield, and when he lifted his wiper up to clean underneath it he got something sticky on his hand. He followed the sign and drove around the back of the building to find the restroom. He parked and went inside to use the facilities. Mister was so nervous because of Matt's questions that when Matt left, Mister didn't see him drive to the back.

Matt came out of the restroom and was ready to hop back in the Jeep when a glint of sunlight caught his attention. It came from a shaded area off the parking lot. He walked back to see what it was, and as he neared the trees he could see a parked vehicle. He removed his sunglasses and saw that it was an old beat up brown Ford truck. Matt took his cell phone out of his pocket and dialed Pete's number. Pete answered on the first ring.

"Pete, good you're there. I need you to run a plate for me. ASAP. It's AHC937, that's Adam-Henry-Charles-937."

Pete said he would call right back.

Maggie had cried herself to sleep in Matt's arms on the couch. When she woke, she was still on the couch with a pillow under her head and a blanket over her. She was wearing the clothes from the night before, and Matt had already gone. She sat up and found a note on the coffee table.

Dear Bert,

All the information for Pete is on the table. Tell him everything, then stay by the phone today and wait for Pete to call back. Don't call me. I'll be tailing Bradley, and I don't want my phone to ring. I'll probably be late so if you need anything call Pete.

Matt

Maggie felt foolish for acting the way she had the night before. She also felt drained and a bit indifferent. It was 6:30 and she felt it would probably be too early to call Pete. She wanted a cup of coffee anyway to help wake her before she spoke to anyone. While the coffee brewed, Maggie took a seat on the deck to look out over the bay. It was a cloudy morning, but warm nonetheless. Somewhere out there was Tracey. It seemed almost impossible that they would find her, but then she and Matt had already accomplished a lot in such a short time.

They knew Bradley was involved, and that he knew where Tracey was. Maggie was sure Matt would make Bradley talk any way he could. She was feeling more positive. The coffee was ready, and she went back inside to pour a cup.

The Cuban's man hid in the tall green foliage on the hillside below the beach house deck. The jungle-like two foot leaves gave him minimal protection from being seen. The deck was built on the hillside, with stilts supporting it to keep it level with the house. When Maggie stepped back inside the house, the man made a run for it and hid underneath the large ten-foot area.

Excitement grew within Maggie as she became more confident that Matt would uncover what Bradley was hiding and find out where Tracey was being held. She decided it was worth a try to see if Pete was in his office and dialed his number. The line was busy, indicating that at least Pete was there. She had several copies to fax him and started sending the information. He would have it in hand when she explained all of it to him.

Chapter 29

Matt was leaning against the Jeep when his phone rang.

"Hello."

"Matt, it's Pete. I've got what you want. That plate comes back to a Harry Burns, 15 Seabreeze Way, St. Thomas. Is there anything else I can do for you?"

"Yeah. Has Maggie called you yet?"

"Not yet."

"She's going to soon. I've got some surveillance to do today, and she has information for you. I told her not to call so my phone doesn't ring. I also told her if she needs anything to call you. Can you hang around the phone today?"

"No problem. I'll tell her when she calls that I'll be here."

"Thanks, Pete.

Matt went back into the station to inquire about the owner of the truck. He used a back door and saw the mechanic first. Mister was still at the pumps taking care of customers.

"Excuse me. I was wondering if you could help me."

The mechanic lifted his head from underneath the hood of a car. "What con I do for you?'

Matt could barely understand him because of his thick dialect. "I was just using the restroom when I noticed an old Ford parked underneath the trees."

"Ya. Dat belong to him." He pointed to Mister.

"Is his name Harry Burns?"

"No mon. Mistar Burns owns de station. He sold de truck to him over a year ago."

He must not have changed the plates, thought Matt.

"It tis old, but we con keep it running smoothly." He smiled, and Matt saw that he was missing two front teeth.

Matt saw Mister coming back inside. "Thanks for the information." He left through the back door so Mister wouldn't see him. It was starting to rain again, and Matt made a dash for his Jeep.

Chapter 30

Maggie had sent all the paperwork to Pete and tried calling him again. The line was still busy, so she poured another cup of coffee and would try again in a few minutes. The rain kept her from going back outside to wait.

The man hiding underneath the deck was protected from the rain, at least until the ground became saturated, then he would be sitting in mud. He hadn't had a chance to check the weather report before leaving his house, and he had no idea how long it was supposed to rain. He heard the beeps from the fax machine inside the house and could hear Maggie shifting about. He assumed she was alone because he had seen Matt drive away earlier.

She tried calling again and this time he answered. "Pete, this is Maggie. I've faxed you pictures that Matt and I found of Tracey, and we think the others are some of the children that have been taken from the islands in past years."

The Cuban's man could hear the one-sided conversation from where he was, even over the gentle tapping of the rain. Roberta Watkins clearly said, "This is Maggie." He thought about the woman he had met three months ago. She had a similar build, but he distinctly remembered her long red hair and Roberta Watkins' hair was short and black.

The wind had changed directions, and Maggie felt a mist coming through the screen door. She stretched the cord as far as it would go, but couldn't reach the door.

"Pete, could you hold on a minute?" She put the receiver on the kitchen counter and went to the sliding door to close it. She left a small crack to let some air inside, then ran back to the phone.

"Sorry. It's starting to rain a bit more, and I had to close the door."

The Cuban's man could only make out part of the conversation now. He moved forward underneath the deck to be closer to the door.

"As I was saying, we found pictures that prove Tracey is alive, but we have no idea where."

Maggie was pacing, walking from the counter to the door. Every time she walked away from the door, the Cuban's man couldn't hear her, making it impossible to understand what she said.

"We went to Bradley's house last night and found everything. He's definitely in on Tracey's disappearance."

"Listen, Maggie. You stay away from him. From what I've learned since I last talked with you, I'm ninety-nine percent sure he killed his wife. He's a dangerous man."

"Do you think Matt's in danger?"

"He knows what he's doing. I talked with him this morning, and he said if you need anything today, you are to call me. I'll be by the phone until I hear from Matt again."

"Thanks, Pete. Please let me know if you come up with anything from the pictures or the copies of Tracey's file."

All Cuban's man could understand was something about pictures, a file, and someone might be in trouble. *Damn rain*, he thought. *It hasn't rained during the day for months, and it has to start today.*

Maggie closed the door all the way. It seemed like the temperature had gone down some. Since she had done all she could for the moment, she decided to take a shower. She had just spoken with Pete, and she knew Matt wouldn't be calling for awhile, so she could take a shower now and would be available if they called later. She closed the other sliding doors before she went into the bathroom.

After the Cuban's man heard Maggie close all the doors, he waited a minute, then peeked around from underneath the deck. The great room was empty, and he was able to see into the first section of the kitchen. She was nowhere in sight, so he jumped onto the deck and crept close to the door. He gently slid the door open and could hear the running water in the shower. He saw the papers, notes and other objects scattered about on the table. Slipping through the door, he took a closer look and saw copies of Tracey's file, the information on the missing kids, and copies of the pictures he had taken at Mister's. *Who the hell are these people?*

The shower water stopped, and the Cuban's man dropped the papers he had in his hand onto the table. He headed back to the door and slipped through just as Maggie was walking out of her bedroom. She had her terrycloth robe on and was rubbing her hair with a towel. She looked up and saw him running from the deck. Startled, she closed the top of her robe with one hand and dropped her towel on the floor. He was gone in an instant. She ran to the door and locked it, at the same time noticing the rainwater lying in a puddle by the door, and followed the trail with her eyes that led to the table. Instinctively, Maggie went to each door and locked them.

Chapter 31

Matt drove around the block and parked in a shopping plaza lot. He walked through the small wooded area to get to the truck. The doors weren't locked and Matt quietly opened the passenger door and jumped inside. He guessed it to be a 1985 Silverado, and in good condition for its age. The bench style seat had two holes, one baseball size hole on the passenger seat and one twice as large in the driver's seat area. A homemade, foam rubber seat cushion covered the larger hole.

Matt picked up the cushion and found underneath it, intertwined in the spring, a badly faded green balloon. He replaced the cushion and felt under the seats with his hand. Unsure that he might be missing something, he held onto the back of the seat with one hand and tipped himself upside down to look under it. All he found was a candy wrapper and a toothpick. He had to admit the truck was old, but clean.

As he pulled himself back up, the bench seat back came forward. Behind the seat he found a tire iron, a small gym bag, a box, and old tattered army blanket. He opened the box first and found it was full of rags, old dishcloths, torn pieces of sheets and pieces of old cloth diapers. When he opened the gym bag, he found the evidence he needed. The bag contained a folded clown suit, a multicolored curly clown wig, a red nose, gloves, and a ziplock bag containing professional face paints.

"It's always the quiet ones," Matt mumbled. It was no wonder why the man at the pumps didn't talk to people, and now Matt knew why he didn't admit to knowing the police chief. *But how are he and Bradley connected?* he wondered. He put things back in order and continued to search.

The glove compartment was locked, so he used one of his picks to open it. Inside was a flashlight, a ball of string, extra truck fuses and an owner's manual. He thumbed through the manual, and an old vehicle registration fell from between two pages that listed Harry Burns as the owner of the truck. Matt replaced everything as it was and locked the compartment. This changed his plans, knowing it would be best to follow the pump assistant today.

Chapter 32

"It's starting to rain more," Tracey told Teodoro, who was looking out the kitchen window with her.

"It should stop later, but it doesn't matter because we're going tonight, no matter what," he told her firmly.

"Look at Jose," Tracey said. Jose was sitting in a rocker in the living room with his feet up in the chair, and his arms around his knees as if any minute the floor would be flooded. "I don't see how we'll ever get him to go."

Teodoro pulled the top part of a bottle out of his pant pocket. "If I have to use this on him, I will."

Tracey looked around to make sure Mama wasn't where she could see or hear them. "What's that?" She didn't know what Teodoro had for sure, but she had her suspicions. "Is that the sleeping liquid?"

Teodoro nodded. "After we talked last night, I went and got it from his truck."

"What if Mister finds out it's missing?"

"He won't, unless he takes somebody today, and I don't think that will happen."

"What do you mean about using it on Jose?"

"I was thinking if he had just a whiff, it might make him tired and he wouldn't fight us."

"Could it make him too tired to walk that far?"

"Maybe. That's why I think he would need only a whiff. Anyway, I'll worry about that when the time comes. Are the girls ready?"

"Yes."

"Good. We will leave as planned, and we *will* make it."

"I know." She smiled. "We can do anything if we put our minds to it."

Chapter 33

The Cuban's man was soaked by the time he got back to his car. He dialed the Cuban, and this time he was going to tell him everything. He was prepared to tell him that there were too many people investigating the abduction of the Brown girl, and if something wasn't done, and done quickly, everyone involved stood a good chance of being caught.

"Your negligence in this matter has put me in a most vulnerable position. My entire operation is in danger because you have lost control." The Cuban had been reprimanding his employee for five minutes. The man was beginning to wonder if his life was in danger.

"I want you to listen very carefully, and I want you to follow my instructions to the letter. I will not tolerate any more insubordination. Comprende?"

"Yes, sir."

"I will send my men to get the children. I will have the Smiths take care of Mister and his wife. Can I trust you to take care of this Maggie Brown and her male companion?"

"Yes, sir."

"I do not care how you do it, but make it quick and make their deaths look like an accident."

"Yes, sir."

He disconnected and looked at the rain rolling down his windshield making hundreds of tiny flowing rivers. *When it rains, it pours,* he thought. He remembered when Mister had called earlier, he told him Watkins, or whoever this man was, had just been at the station. He started his car and drove toward town, assuming Watkins would still be around asking questions. He would stop by his house first and change from his wet clothes into his work clothes.

Although the condition created by the two men in St. John had certainly jeopardized his operation, the Cuban had taken care of worse situations. He would handle this matter as he had in the past with similar circumstances.

"I want you to go to Culebra Island and collect the children. Bring them here, put them in the west wing, and tomorrow I will have each of them picked up and taken to separate facilities. Take them any way you need to," demanded the Cuban. His right-hand man listened carefully to his boss of thirty years.

"And I want you to go get the Smiths. Let them think you are taking them to the island to eliminate Mister and his wife. Bradley has instructions to meet you there when he has finished killing Maggie Brown and her friend. I want you to kill all of them and leave them there. I don't want any loose ends. Bradley has put all of us in danger and we must clean up his mess."

Chapter 34

It had rained all day, and the forecast wasn't good. A storm was moving in from the east and was to hit the islands around midnight. When the phone rang, Maggie looked at her watch. It was 4:02 p.m. and she hadn't heard from Matt. She ran from the bedroom to answer the phone in the kitchen.

"Hello."

"Maggie Brown?" The voice on the phone sounded muffled.

"Yes?"

"I know where your daughter is. You must meet me at the Annaberg Ruins at 9:00 tonight. Do you know where that is?"

"Yes."

She heard the click.

"Wait." But it was too late; the party had disconnected.

Maggie wanted to call Matt, but he told her specifically not to call, and she didn't want to put him in danger. She did as she was told and dialed Pete. The line was busy and she hung up.

Maggie knew she had no choice but to meet with the stranger who called. She dialed Pete's number again. This time it was ringing.

"Hello."

"Oh, thank God. Pete, you're there."

Pete could hear the urgency in her voice. "Maggie, what's wrong?"

"I just received a call from a man who says he knows where Tracey is and wants me to meet with him tonight."

"Have you heard from Matt?"

"No, and I can't call him. What do I do?"

"You can't go."

"I don't see how I can *not* go."

"It could be a trap, Maggie, and you'd be alone. You'd be a sitting duck. This kind of situation is for professionals."

"This could be my only chance to find out where she is, and if I don't go, then what?"

"I don't know. Maybe he'll call back when Matt's there."

"Pete, you know I can't take that chance."

Pete thought for a moment. "What does Matt think of Wells?"

"He hasn't said much really, why?"

"It might be a good idea to call him in on this."

"What if he tries to stop me?"

"Then if you don't call Wells, you must call Matt."

"And risk putting him in danger, no way."

Pete could hear Maggie's determination, but made one last attempt to change her mind. "It wouldn't be as dangerous as you going alone. What time are you to meet?"

"Nine o'clock." Maggie remembered the Jeep rentals closed at 5:00. "Pete, I don't even have a car."

"What do you mean?" Pete was relieved to know Maggie didn't have a way to get around.

"Matt has my rental. When he came, I picked him up, and we've only had one vehicle since."

"Okay. So now you'll have to call Matt."

Maggie thought for a moment then lied, "I'll call him right away."

"Then have him call me."

Maggie didn't answer; she was too busy thinking about how she could get to the rental facility.

"Maggie, are you listening?" Pete interrupted her thoughts.

"Yes, Pete."

"You'll have Matt call me?"

"Yes."

"Promise me."

"Yes, I promise."

Maggie knew what she had to do. She was not going to put Matt in more danger by calling him, and she needed a way to get around. She went to the kitchen and looked by the phone for Claire Turner's number.

"Hello," Claire answered.

"Claire, this is Maggie Brown. I need a favor."

Claire was there in twenty minutes and drove Maggie to town to the Jeep rental. They arrived just before closing.

"Now remember, miss, you must drive on de left side of de road."

Maggie thanked the rental owner and drove to the station to fill the tank with gas. Little did she know, Matt was just a block away. Mister took her money for the gas, and she headed back to the Bayview. She knew meeting the man alone was a stupid thing to do, but she felt she had no other choice. She had to do it for Tracey's sake.

When Maggie returned to the beach house, she was afraid to go inside. Since the afternoon's weird events with the strange man on the deck, noises and sudden moves made her look twice and react on impulse. She knew if she was going to make it through the night she would have to get a grip and settle down. She locked the door behind her and went to the bathroom for a towel. It was still raining, and she had gotten wet running from the Jeep to the door. She shed her jacket, patted dry with the towel and fluffed her curly hair lightly, letting it air dry.

The answering machine light was flashing, indicating she had messages. She pushed the button and listened. There were three messages from Pete to call him right away, and one message confirmed their suspicions about Ivan Price. Pete said Price had told the LA cops that Bradley had paid him to leave town for awhile until he could close the case on the missing girl. Bradley didn't elaborate and Price didn't ask questions, he just took the money and ran.

Maggie wished Matt was there so he could hear the message and to be with her when she met the anonymous caller. It was ironic for her to think just a few days ago she hadn't relied on anyone, and now she was afraid to make a move without asking Matt. She knew she could, and would do what she had to do alone, but the comfort of having someone with her was appealing. Maggie wasn't going to call Pete back. That way she wouldn't have to lie to him and tell him she wasn't going.

Chapter 35

The Smiths were very unhappy about going out on such a night. The weather was getting worse each hour, raining constantly, with wind gusts up to thirty miles per hour.

They met the Cuban's boat and his men on the docks at St. Thomas, who were going to transport them across to St. John to do the job. Mr. Smith wondered why the other men couldn't do the job, then he and his wife could go home, but he also knew they couldn't refuse the job because the Cuban would have them killed.

"I'm afraid, Mr. Smith." Mrs. Smith stood on the dock, clenching her coat closed in the wind.

"Why don't you stay here? I can do this alone, dear."

One of the Cuban's men took Mrs. Smith by the arm and forced her to step on the fifty-eight foot Criss Craft boat. Mr. Smith took his wife to the shelter of the cutty cabin.

"I fear we are in great danger, my husband."

"I think you're right. We'll have to watch and get away when we can."

Chapter 36

Matt had fallen asleep in his Jeep waiting for Mister to get off work. He assumed Mister would be putting in a full day's work, but he wanted to stay close to him in case he went somewhere. Matt checked his watch—6:00. The sky was dark and the wind was blowing, but it had stopped raining for the moment. From the dark clouds in the sky, Matt knew it would be raining again soon. At 6:15 he saw the lights go out at the station, and Mister wheel the displays inside. He was in his truck and on the road by 6:20, and Matt was tailing behind.

Matt had come prepared with an all-weather jacket. The temperature had dropped another ten degrees. He had listened to the weather report on the radio on the ferry ride to Culebra Island while following Mister. The forecaster predicted a storm to come into the islands around midnight, and Matt was hoping to be indoors somewhere by that time, knowing that tropical storms could be vicious.

He parked the Jeep on top of the hill, near the clump of trees, out of sight from the farmhouse. Before he got out, he made sure he had his gun, flashlight, cell phone and stungun. His coat served not only as a protector from the elements, but a carryall as well. He kept his light pointed on the ground to see where he was walking and so that the light wouldn't be detected from a distance. A small shiny object on the ground caught his eye. He picked it up and held the round cigar band in his hand. *Bradley's been here too,* he thought. He put the band in his pocket and began down the hillside. When he got to the barn, the guard dog greeted him, but Matt had come prepared for a situation like that too.

"Come on, buddy, come see Matt." He coaxed the dog to him. The dog didn't hesitate, and lunged forward, attacking Matt. Matt held his stungun out in front of him and with one zap the dog was on the ground, motionless.

He took a small ball of string from the front zipper pocket in his pullover jacket and tied the string around the dog's nose and then anchored it around his head, making a string muzzle, so that the dog couldn't bark or bite. He wrapped string around the dog's front and hind legs. Matt saw an old rusted horseshoe stake near the compost pile and tied the dog to it, wrapping the string several times around the dog's collar and the stake. The dog was tied so many different ways that even when he regained his strength, he wouldn't be able to move.

Matt made his way to the side of the house and walked its perimeter to have a look around. The upstairs of the house was dark and didn't have curtains at any of the windows, and it appeared that no one used that part of the house. The ground level had a dining area-turned living room, a room with five beds, another room with four beds and a kitchen where all the children had gathered. He could see they were getting ready to eat. He wasn't able to get a good look from where he was standing, so he moved around to the side of the house and tried to see more through the kitchen window. He could see all the children in the room except a girl who was squatted beside a smaller girl. She stood and turned toward the kitchen window, and Matt could clearly see it was Tracey. He quickly ducked below the window and out of sight.

Chapter 37

Maggie drove with care along the slippery wet winding roads. St. John's hairpin turns became even more dangerous when they were wet. It wasn't that she was concerned with her own driving in such weather, as she was with another driver with lesser skills. She fought the steering wheel against wind gusts. Checking her watch, she found she had ten minutes to get to the sugar ruins.

Maggie and Tracey had gone to the ruins in July, and Maggie knew the area well. Sitting on top of a mountain, the ruins spread across a two acre area. There wasn't much left in most of the buildings, just a few stone walls. A native lady baked sugar cakes, demonstrating how it would have been made two hundred years ago.

Tracey had been particularly interested in the basket weaver who sat in front of one of the ruins weaving a large basket in her lap, made of colorfully dyed strips of reed. The lady wore a wide brimmed straw hat to shelter her dark skin from the sun, a cotton gingham print dress, and a pair of huraches. Tracey had asked the lady if she could take her picture, and she had willingly said yes.

Even on high speed, Maggie's windshield wipers weren't moving fast enough to clear away the rain, so she had to slow down to twenty miles per hour. It was raining so hard, and it was so dark, she could only see ten feet in front of her, and her headlights didn't seem to help. Someone came up behind her at one point and passed as if she were driving too slowly. She guessed it was a local who was accustomed to such weather and the winding roads.

The windows on the inside of the Jeep were beginning to fog over. Maggie turned the defroster on high and wiped the windshield with her hand. Just as she finished clearing the area in front of her, she looked up and saw a Jeep sitting sideways in the middle of a hairpin curve. She grabbed the wheel with both hands, and when she swerved to miss the Jeep, there was no place to go except off the road.

The tires hit the rocky edge of the road and she stomped on the brakes. The Jeep skidded along the sand and sent Maggie and her Jeep down the side of a mountain. The Jeep's tire hit a large rock, bouncing Maggie off her seat, and she hit the top of the ragtop, jamming her neck. Her seatbelt tightened, making it hard for her to breathe. The front of the Jeep hit a tree, and Maggie's door flew open, snapping off at the hinges. The Jeep continued to tumble downhill.

She hit a larger tree, sending the Jeep in a sideways rolling motion. Without protection from the door, Maggie hit the ground several times and was jerked around like a rag doll. The last sound she heard was the crushing sound of metal hitting the tree that finally stopped the tumbling. Her head hit the windshield with a thud.

The Cuban's man raised his flashlight above his head and looked down the mountainside. "One down, one to go." He sneered.

Chapter 38

Matt knew he wasn't going to leave Culebra and get back to St. John tonight. Even if he could find a water taxi, he was sure the weather was too bad for them to take a chance getting across. The wind had picked up tremendously since he had arrived. He decided to find a place in the barn to hide until morning, then he would call Maggie and seek help freeing Tracey.

Matt opened the barn door and used his flashlight to look around inside. He saw the dog in the pen. He barely lifted his head as Matt examined him from a distance. Matt could tell by looking that the animal had suffered a traumatic experience and wouldn't be a threat to him.

Mister's truck was parked in the middle of the barn, and Matt knew he would have to leave the barn before Mister came out in the morning to go to work. He would call the St. Thomas police department for backup after the man went to work and use them to help free the children.

He looked around inside and saw bags of pig feed, dog food, bales of hay, and many other supplies. When he got to the box, he opened the hinged roof to look inside. A tiny three-footed stool sat inside, and nothing else. Using his flashlight, he could see drawings carved into the wood siding. He saw stick-figure people, swings, houses, trees, flowers and balls. Matt's stomach became queasy with the thought that a child might have spent time in the small area. He closed the lid and continued looking elsewhere.

He shined his light up to the loft, then used the wooden ladder to climb there. When he looked in one of the corners, he found Teodoro's raft. It looked like the raft was new construction by the extra boards and cut pieces of rawhide laying about. Matt remembered when he was a boy building a similar raft to float on the river by his house. He wondered if the children had built this one and how they planned to use it.

Matt felt the excruciating blow from the metal gun butt that hit the back of his head, but didn't realize what hit him. He fell to his knees. His head was bleeding and ached with pain. He turned to face his attacker and saw Bradley standing over him, his gun pointed at his face.

"Mr. Watkins, or whoever you are, you are on private property and I'm afraid you're trespassing. I must take you into custody." Bradley patted Matt down and took his gun, stungun and cell phone.

"I think you should check with the owner and you'll find out I've been invited here," Matt bluffed Bradley.

"That's peculiar. I know the owner, and he has no idea you're here."

"Since we each have different viewpoints on the situation, why don't we call him and his family outside and see which one of us is right?"

"Why don't we stop playing this game and get to the point?" Bradley became serious. "Are you surprised to see me?'

"No, not really. I know a bad cop when I see one. I was wondering when you'd make your move." Matt touched the back of his neck and felt the fresh blood.

"Surely Watkins isn't your real name. Who are you?" Bradley asked.

"You're not even a good-bad cop. Haven't you figured that out yet?'

Matt's sarcasm irritated Bradley and made him angry. He lifted his foot, kicking Matt in the mouth, making him fall backward.

Matt shook it off and stood up. His bottom lip had been cut by the edge of his tooth, and he wiped the blood off with his sleeve.

"You might as well tell me your real name. This will be the last time you have a chance to say it." Bradley smiled sinisterly.

"Are you sure you don't mean this is the last time you'll hear it? I know the kids are here, and I know the man inside the house has taken them, but what's your part in all this? My guess it that you're working for someone. I hope your pay is enough, but I'll bet they live better than you." Matt could see Bradley getting heated. "I figure you have a key to the Otigas' and you messed up the chief's office, took the Brown file and killed the chief. For what?"

"Yeah, okay, smart man. You're trespassing and it's my job to keep the law. I'd read you your rights, but a dead man can't go to jail. Oh, yes, and your friend, is it, Maggie Brown? She won't be going anywhere ever again." Bradley sneered.

Now Bradley had Matt's attention.

"You see, she had an awful accident tonight, poor thing. I guess our terrible weather caused her to slip off the road and down a mountainside."

"That's odd," Matt said, calling Bradley's bluff. "Maggie didn't have a Jeep to drive."

Bradley became cockier and started speaking like a cop. "At approximately 17:00 hours, the victim rented a vehicle in town. Then, at

20:00 hours, said victim left her beach house, known as the Bayview, with every intention of meeting an anonymous caller who said he knew where her daughter was being held. Unfortunately, she met an obstacle in the road, forcing her to swerve and lose control of her rented vehicle. Approximate time of death, 18:20 hours."

Matt was furious and lunged at Bradley, catching him off guard and knocking the gun from his hand, over the edge of the loft and onto the barn floor. The men struggled, each one trying to get control of the other. Matt punched Bradley in the nose and twisted his arm behind him. He tried to stand and force Bradley to do the same, but Bradley turned and in a split second was free from Matt's strong grip. He came toward Matt and punched him in the stomach, forcing Matt to double over. Bradley wound up to throw another punch, but Matt saw it coming and stood to the side. Matt jumped on top of him, and the two men rolled, hooked together.

The force of their body weights was in control and in one quick instance, the men fell over the side of the loft and into the bed of Mister's truck. Bradley was on the bottom and had the air knocked out of him. This gave Matt the advantage. He knelt over Bradley, holding him up by his shirt, then punched him in the face. The back of Bradley's head hit the truck as Matt let go. He tried to push Matt away, but Matt held him down. Bradley freed one arm and stretched as far sideways as he could. Using his fingertips, he managed to grasp the knife he had strapped to his ankle. Lifting his hand, he cut Matt's arm just below his shoulder.

Matt jumped up to get away from the knife, but it was too late. Bradley grabbed Matt by his injured arm and swung him around, throwing him into a sitting position. He held his knife at Matt's throat. Bradley pulled handcuffs from his back pocket and snapped one side of the cuffs around Matt's wrist, pulling him forward by the cuffs, all the while holding the knife to his neck.

"Get up," Bradley ordered.

Matt got to his feet, then Bradley cuffed Matt's other hand behind his back. The two men struggled to regain normal breathing. Bradley took Matt's wallet from his pocket and searched for Matt's true identity. He located his New York driver's license.

"Matt Sanford, that your real name? Let's see what else I can find." He pulled another card that revealed Matt's PI status. "So, the late Ms. Brown hired you to find her daughter? Well," Bradley laughed, "you did what you were hired to do, but a bit late I'm afraid."

Matt stalled for time to try and figure out a way to get free. "You know, it's not too late to turn this around. After all, he's the one with Tracey, not you."

"Yeah, sure. And I'll just walk away."

"Something like that. I could put in a good word, make it easier on you."

"Let's go." He tugged on Matt's bleeding arm, leading him out of the barn.

It was 9:45 and everyone inside the house had gone to bed as usual, but the children lay awake waiting to leave. The storm hadn't slowed, and the wind gusts were still fierce.

Matt realized he was in trouble, and Tracey was in more danger now because Bradley was smart enough to know even if he managed to get rid of Maggie and him, someone else would follow to find out what happened to them, and Matt knew Pete would be the one to come. Bradley took Matt to an old unused outhouse and handcuffed him to the inside.

"It won't do you any good to yell. No one will hear you over the storm, but at least you'll have a place to sit."

His sense of humor eluded Matt as he looked around to find a way out.

"After the storm I'll take you back to St. John and deposit you with your friend, and it will look like you died in the crash together. Those Jeeps are tricky to drive on a wet slippery road." He laughed and left Matt.

Bradley fought the wind back to the barn where he located a ragged blanket and curled up in a corner to sleep for a couple of hours. He knew his night was not over yet.

Chapter 39

Maggie felt the rainwater run down her face and opened her eyes. It was dark and the blow to her head had temporarily impaired her sight. She had a three inch gash along her hairline from when her head had hit the windshield. Raising her hand to it, she felt the fresh blood. A hand touched hers and she jerked with surprise.

"Miss Maggie Brown?"

"Yes," she managed to squeak. "Who's there?"

"You will be all right. I have come to help you." The man's thick dialect told her it was an islander and somehow soothed her.

The rain was still coming down and Maggie could feel it on her left side. She blinked a few times and her vision began to clear. The Jeep was lying on its side, and the only thing holding her in place was her seatbelt.

"We are on de side of a mountain, and it tis raining, so we must move quickly, but carefully as well, so dat de Jeep does not slide down hill any further." The man sounded confident, and put Maggie at ease. "Con you understand me?"

"Yes."

"When I tell you, try to unfasten de seatbelt and I will pull you out."

Maggie realized then that the Jeep was facing straight downward, and the man was standing behind her, leaning backward, almost as if he took another step forward, he would lose his balance. He took her arm and moved it around a bit.

"Does anyting hurt when I move your arm?"

"No."

"Dats good. Are you ready?"

"Yes."

"I will count to three and den you unfasten de belt."

She fumbled with her right hand, trying to locate the release button. Her hand shook as she pushed it gently, making sure it would depress.

"One, two, three."

Maggie pushed, and the man pulled with such force the two of them fell to the ground. Maggie heard a loud crack as the tree that was holding the Jeep in place broke in half. The Jeep shifted and started to slide forward. The man had his foot pushed tightly against a tree limb, and that was the only thing keeping the two of them from sliding along with the Jeep. The Jeep slid intermittently a few inches, and then in one smooth slide went sailing off the side of the cliff, floating downward in midair off the side of the mountain. Maggie saw then that they were only a few inches away from the edge, and that the Jeep had been teetering on the edge the entire time.

She laid on her back on top of her rescuer, his large hands holding her by her arms to keep her from sliding.

"Are you all right?" he asked.

"Yes, I think so." Maggie's body ached with pain.

"We must walk up de mountain, con you make it?"

"Yes, I'll try."

They used branches and the ground to find footing. He put an arm around her waist and put her arm around his neck.

"Looks like we got you out just in time." He smiled.

She looked up and recognized her dance partner Dario Raz.

She took a couple of steps and fell to the ground. She was too dizzy to walk and felt she would pass out. The tall muscular Mr. Raz picked her up and carried her like a child up the side of the mountain.

Chapter 40

Pete checked the clock on the office wall: 8:20, which would be 9:20 St. John time. He was nervous about Maggie not answering his messages. He knew Maggie was headstrong and was afraid she had gone to meet with the caller. Calling Matt was out of the question. He tossed around the idea of calling Wells. Pete suspected Bradley might have been the caller, which meant Maggie was already in serious trouble. If Wells was in on it, calling him wouldn't make any difference. In fact, it might help, letting him know someone else knew what was going on. His investigation hadn't shown any evidence that Wells shouldn't be trusted, and his gut feeling told him Wells was one of the good guys.

The dispatcher answered on the first ring. Pete didn't think Wells would be in the office at this hour. He knew he would have to be careful what he told the dispatcher so he didn't draw any questionable interest in his call. He didn't want anyone except Wells to know why he was calling.

"My name is Pete Sanford, and I'm calling from New York. I need to get in touch with Robert Wells. Is he there by any chance?"

"No, it tis too late and he is at home. Con I help you with someting?" she asked.

Pete knew most police officers had unlisted numbers, and it wasn't customary for the departments to give those numbers to the public, so he asked if there was a way to get in touch with him instead of asking for his number.

"Would you like de number?"

"Yeah, sure." Pete scrambled for a pencil, surprised that she would relinquish the number. He dialed the number immediately and found Wells at home. He started by telling Wells who he was, and that Maggie was in immediate danger. Wells called Pete back on his cell phone as he drove to the sugar ruins. He listened as Pete told the entire story. Pete learned that Wells had never cared for Bradley's work methods, and even though Bradley had closed the chief's case, Wells had continued to work on it secretly. Pete also informed Wells about the Smiths at that point.

“So Bradley must have had something to do with the Smiths getting away too?” Wells suggested. “What made you decide to trust me?”

“Desperation and urgency to tell the truth. Of course, your record is clean, unlike Bradley’s, but we weren’t sure you weren’t working with him until now,” Pete answered.

“Is…the…any…you…contac…help you?

“You’re breaking up,” Pete said. “It must be the storm,” and Wells was gone.

Pete hung up the phone and kept the line clear for Maggie, Matt or Wells.

Chapter 41

Maggie opened her eyes and looked around. She was lying on a couch in a darkened room and could hear voices. When she sat up, her head pounded and her body ached. She looked toward the voices, and saw three people sitting around a kitchen table. One was Dario Raz.

"Feeling bettah, Miss Brown?" asked Raz.

"Like a truck hit me."

Everyone laughed.

"Please join us." Raz pushed the seat next to him out with his foot, and Maggie went to sit beside him.

"Con I get you a cup of tea?" asked one of the women.

"Yes, thank you."

The woman went to the stove and turned on a gas burner, setting a kettle of water on top of the flame.

"Dat is Selena, and dis is Carey," introduced Raz.

Everyone exchanged hellos, and Maggie wondered about the relationship of the three. Selena looked to be in her twenties, Carey in her thirties and Raz in his fifties.

"Selena and Carey are sistahs and share dis house. I am just a friend." The women snickered.

"How did you know that's what I was thinking?"

"Raz knows almost everyting. Of course, he con not read de mind, but he knows many tings," Carey said.

Selena brought Maggie her tea, set it in front of her, and with a quirky smile said, "Be sure to drink all of it."

"She will be needing milk, Selena," Raz added.

Maggie's questionable look prompted Raz to answer. "Just a hunch."

The women laughed. The way they seemed to know what each other was thinking seemed a bit creepy to Maggie. Maggie heard a clock chime and was suddenly aware of the time. She looked for her watch, but it was gone.

"What time is it?" Her urgency was obvious.

Raz answered without looking at a clock. "It tis 9:30, but not to worry. Your mystery mon will not be at de ruins."

She looked surprised. "How do you know about that?"

Selena put her hand on Maggie's shoulder. "Raz is a Rasta Shephard, Miss Brown.

"A Rasta Shepherd?" Maggie seemed confused.

Selena continued. "He is our leader, our healer, our preacher, and a prophet. Raz has great clairvoyant powers and has helped many people."

Maggie had witnessed the respect given to Raz by the locals, and now when the woman spoke about him, she could feel the power he entertained.

"How did you find me?"

"I was walking in de woods and heard de crash. You are very lucky to be alive."

Selena took her seat at the table after handing Maggie the milk. Maggie poured some in her tea and continued questioning.

Maggie thought how strange it was for him to be walking during the storm, but didn't question him about it.

"Did you see any of the accident?" she asked.

"What I saw was not an accident. You were meant to die in de crash tonight."

"What do you mean?"

"De Jeep was placed in de road on purpose—for you, Miss Brown."

"How do you know?"

Raz scooted forward in his chair and put his arm on the table. Looking directly into Maggie's eyes, he said, "Raymond Bradley tried to kill you tonight."

Raz caught Maggie off guard. "Tried to kill me? Why does he want me dead?"

"You are interfering in his business and getting too close to de truth. Bradley is an evil mon who has authority as an officah on de island. Dis is a dangerous mix."

Maggie saw the two women had become serious.

Raz continued. "He has hidden many secrets from Chief Otiga in de past."

"You knew the chief?"

"Yes, very well."

Maggie thought for a minute, then blurted out, "Can you help me find my daughter?"

"I have been helping de chief for over a month. And now I will help you. Rastafarians have gathered at the tabernacle to pray for forgiveness in hopes de storm will subside. We will join them and see what we con do."

Raz stood and the women followed. When Maggie was studying world art, she had read a little about the Rastafarians and their religion and realized Raz was their leader. Many leaders were chosen because of their extrasensory perception and clairvoyant abilities. When Maggie had gone back to New York after Tracey's disappearance, she received a call from a lady who claimed to have ESP and wanted to help find Tracey. Maggie dismissed it as nonsense and had never contacted the woman. Today, she was open to anything, and Raz had a presence she couldn't ignore.

The church was nothing more than a pole barn built over a cement slab floor, with wooden window covers that were hinged at the top and propped open with long boards. The building reminded Maggie of the camp pavilion that they had used when she was a Girl Scout. Approximately fifty people were gathered inside the church. Some people sat in folding chairs, others danced in a formed circle, some were playing drums or singing, and the rest were gathered at a primitive altar.

Raz walked inside, raised his hands and lifted his head to look above. One woman met him on his way to the circle with an elaborate turban made of cotton cloth and decorated with braided jute and gemstones. He leaned to the side, and the woman placed the turban on his head. His many dreadlocks hung from underneath, falling around his shoulders to the center of his back. A man came to him and placed a long beige scarf around his neck and over his extended arms. With his arms out to the side, Maggie thought he resembled the massive twenty-one foot statue, Christ of the Caribbean, that stood on the mountaintop on St. John that overlooked the islands.

People came to him, bowed, and touched his scarf. Selena took a spot in the circle and started dancing. Carey took Maggie's hand and led her to a chair, then sat beside her. The circle parted, and Raz stood in the middle, slowly turning the opposite direction of the circle.

"We have a friend in need with us tonight, Brothars and Sistars. She is looking for her daughtah," Raz announced.

"De people have formed a trumpeting circle," Carey explained. "Dey will dance to de drums and in the end, gods and spirits will speak through dese people, revealing joys and dangers. It tis within de circle dat insight to your daughtar's whereabouts may be revealed."

"Should I be doing something?" asked Maggie.

"Noting yet. Raz will come for you when he is ready."

The circle became bigger as eight more people took a place next to the others. Maggie felt out of place being the only Caucasian in the room and not knowing what was happening. She thought about the turn of events within the past twenty-four hours and where they had taken her. She was feeling helpless where Tracey was concerned, and she felt she had lost Matt's respect for the choices she'd made about raising Tracey. She had lied to Pete, and her self-esteem was slipping away fast.

The roar of the rain pounding on the metal roof added to the steady beat of the drums. People chanted and people sang. The room was hot and humid from the body heat and the storm. Maggie began to feel like she had too much to drink. Her eyelids felt heavy and she was lightheaded. Her hands and feet tingled as she sat slumped in the chair. She looked at Carey, who moved freely to the music.

Carey caught her glance. "De tea must be taking effect."

"What?" Maggie said slowly.

"Raz is also a medicine man. Your tea was blended of herbs used to help you heal. You may be feeling disoriented now, but dat will pass."

Raz motioned for Carey to bring Maggie to the center of the circle. It seemed to Maggie that the two of them floated across the floor. Raz took her arms and held them out to her side, her back to the front of him, and they spun in a slow circle, still opposite from the direction of the outer circle of people.

Her face flushed from the warmth and then her body began to sweat, as though she was standing in a sauna. She felt the moisture slip down the small of her back. Maggie closed her eyes and hung her head. The rhythm of the drums and the melodious tones of the music swept over her like a concert orchestra. She mindlessly swayed to the beat.

Images flashed through her mind as if she were watching a play unfold on the stage under a strobe light. She saw an image of the gas station attendant and a lady standing beside the Smiths inside an old house. She saw men dressed in black wearing bulletproof vests carrying guns. An image of Matt rolling on the floor with Bradley came to mind, then she saw Bradley pulling Matt away in handcuffs. The words Triumphant Force were visible to her. The last images she saw were that of Tracey. She saw her walking against the wind in the storm with several other children to the ocean's edge.

The drums stopped, Raz stopped, the circle stopped, and the room was silent for a second. Maggie fell on her knees and opened her eyes. She heard the rain against the roof. The people forming the circle leaned inward and began to babble and speak in tongues. Maggie watched as eyes rolled to the back of the heads, people shook, and people jumped—all were speaking at the same time but saying very different things.

Raz went to one person at a time to listen to what they were saying. He placed his hands on the person's cheeks and the person spoke rapidly. When the person was done, Raz nodded and went onto the next person until he had been with everyone in the circle. Maggie watched and remained kneeling until he was with the last person.

Raz came to Maggie and helped her up from the floor. Maggie was now feeling awake and very much alert.

"It tis not only myself dat possesses clairvoyant powers. De people here have many great powers and con see tings most people connot."

Maggie fully understood after experiencing visions herself.

"Your daughter is in great danger tonight from de storm. She is on an island not far from here. It is called Culebra."

"I know where that is," Maggie said excitedly.

"Dere is a farm house two miles from de shore just past de marina. De mon you have brought wit you is in much danger also, but not from de storm. Raymond Bradley is planning to kill him and dere is little time."

"I must get there then."

Raz took her hand and stopped her from leaving immediately. "Dere is another strong force coming from somewhere. An evil force, but dis was not clear to me. You must watch every step you take and be very careful."

She put her hand on top of his and felt a strong sense of power surge through her that gave her a second wind. "I understand. Thank you."

Raz motioned to one of the men and told him to take Maggie wherever she wanted to go. Maggie walked through the doors of Raz's tabernacle with renewed faith, a boost in confidence, and a definite direction.

Chapter 42

"Pssst."

Tracey heard Moises' signal for the girls to come. Evita was in bed with her, and the two got out and went to the bedroom window. Evita smiled at Moises as Tracey handed her through the window. All the girls were told to remain silent until Teodoro told them to speak, and Evita liked playing the game with her friends.

The boys were standing inside the barn door when the girls and Moises joined them. Rainwater dripped off all the children. Teodoro handed Nalda a flashlight and whispered instructions.

"I found this on the floor." Teodoro was holding Matt's flashlight that he had dropped during his scuffle with Bradley. "It works and we'll take it with us," he told Nalda. "You'll be in charge of the light. You stay beside me, and we'll lead the way. Everyone else follows. I'll carry one side of the raft, Jose and Tobias will take turns carrying the other. Evita stays with Tracey. Any questions?"

Everyone nodded and smiled when Teodoro used Tracey's name. Teodoro went out the barn door first, looking in both directions to make sure no one was there. All the children followed after his signal. The wind was blowing so hard that the children had to fight to walk. Tracey held on tightly to Evita's small hand.

Bradley was huddled in a corner opposite the barn door and covered completely with the blanket, making it impossible for the children to see him. He hadn't slept for two days and was sleeping so soundly that he didn't hear the children.

As they walked around the side of the barn, Teodoro looked for the dog. He expected it to come any minute and was ready with the liquid, meatloaf and rag. He didn't know the dog was tied to the horseshoe stake on the other side of the barn.

Moises walked next to Tracey. "How did Teodoro get Jose to come?"

"He said he would put him to sleep with the sleeping liquid and carry him. I guess he didn't like that idea." Moises smiled with the thought that Teodoro had tricked Jose.

After walking a while, Moises took a squirt from his inhalator so he could breathe. Fighting to walk in the storm and escaping had caused him to have an asthma attack.

"Do you need to stop, Moises?" Tracey asked.

"It's a little hard to breathe, but I'll be fine. I just want to get out of here."

Tracey patted Moises on the back. She felt a tug on her shirt. Evita was in silent tears. Tracey stopped and squatted beside her. "Evita, what is it?" She didn't answer, and Tracey realized no one told her it was all right to speak. "You can talk now."

"I can't walk anymore. It's too hard."

Tracey picked her up and held her close. Evita wrapped her arms and legs around Tracey and laid her head on Tracey's shoulder. Although Tracey didn't mind carrying Evita, she wondered how long she would be able to keep her strength. The children walked against the wind with their wet clothing clinging to their bodies.

A gust of wind tore the raft from the boys' hands and it flew backward, hitting Freiza on the shoulder as it went past. She dropped to the ground wincing with pain.

Nalda ran to her side. "Freiza are you hurt?"

"My arm, my arm," she cried. Freiza rolled on the ground, holding her arm.

Teodoro and Tobias ran after the raft while the other children huddled around Freiza. The boys dragged the raft back to the others.

"Is Freiza hurt?" Teodoro asked.

The noise of the wind and rain made it hard for the children to hear each other without shouting. "She can't move her arm," yelled Juana.

"Can she go on?" he asked.

"Maybe we could tie her arm against her body," Tracey suggested.

Teodoro used his pocketknife and cut the bottom off of Tobias' shirt, then cut it in half. He gave the piece of cloth to Nalda and asked her to use it to bind Frieza's arm to her body. Tracey pulled Teodoro aside.

"I think her arm is broken. It looks like her arm and shoulder are starting to swell."

"I'll have Tobias walk with her to help her along."

Jose and Teodoro continued to carry the raft, but walked behind the children this time. Nalda and Tracey took turns using the flashlight and carrying Evita. Moises used his inhalator often and Tobias was fearful the rain would not stop and they would be caught in a flood. Frieza's broken arm became more painful with every step she took.

Chapter 43

Raz's friend drove Maggie to the Coast Guard office in Cruz Bay as Maggie had requested. She was going to ask the Coast Guard to take her to Culebra Island and help get Tracey. Water dripped from her hair onto the counter in the station. The office was air-conditioned, Maggie was soaking wet, and the combination left her cold and shivering. The two Coast Guardsmen inside had their backs to the door and were busy across the room watching the weather report on the television and didn't notice her come inside.

"Excuse me," she called.

The men turned and looked her way.

"Hello," answered the younger man as he came to the counter. "You're all wet."

He appeared to be twenty or so, had blond wavy hair, blue eyes and a bright white smile that gleamed against his youthful bronze tan. "What can I do for you?"

His co-worker threw a towel to him as if it had been planned before she came through the door. Maggie took the towel and talked as she dried herself.

"I need your help," she started. "I don't have time to tell you the entire story, so I'll give you the short version. Three months ago my daughter was kidnapped, and I just found out she is being held on Culebra Island and I need your help getting there now."

The young man stared at her, suddenly aware of her worn condition and of the long cut on her forehead.

"Can you take me there?"

"Tonight?"

"Yes, now."

"Ma'am, we're in the middle of a tropical storm watch issued by the National Hurricane Center in Florida. There's no way we can take a boat out tonight."

Maggie's red-haired temper started to erupt. "Listen, son. I've been through one horrible day, with a frightening phone call, to a horrendous car accident, where I found out someone was trying to kill me. I'm not in the mood for you or anybody else to tell me that a little rough weather is going to stop me now." She threw the wet towel on the countertop.

The older man, and ranking officer, came to his co-worker's assistance. "Have you called the authorities?"

"They are not around and can't be trusted. I need *you* to get me there."

"I'm sorry, but it is forbidden by the Coast Guard for us to launch a boat in a tropical storm. Even if we wanted to take you out on our own time, it would be a suicide mission. It's near impossible to steer a boat in this wind. Perhaps if you'd like to wait for an hour or two, the storm should have blown out of this region then."

The telephone rang and the younger man went across the room to answer it. The ranking officer continued to talk, but Maggie knew there was no way either of these men were going to help her. She looked around as he talked and saw a keyboard on the wall near the counter. Each key had a tag attached to it with a number on the tag. *It must be a boat or boat slip*, she thought.

"...so when the weather clears up we will be more than happy to help you get to Culebra."

A voice came over the marine radio. "This is Red Hook Coast Guard in St. Thomas. Do you copy, St. John?"

The man turned his head to look at the radio, then looked back at Maggie. "Excuse me, ma'am. I must answer that."

He left her at the counter and went to the radio near the window across the room.

Both men were busy and looking out the large window facing the docks. Maggie inched her way to the end of the counter, not wanting to draw attention her way. When she reached the keyboard, she looked for the highest number, assuming the slips with the higher numbers were to the end of the dock. She grabbed the #10 and ran out the door.

When the men heard the door, they turned and saw she was leaving. Maggie ran to the end dock, reading each slip number as she went past. She was right and #10 was the last boat and slip. All the boats were docked facing outward, which was to her benefit. All she needed to do was untie the ropes and drive away. The numbered boats were Coast Guard rentals, eighteen feet long with inboard/outboard motors. She had done plenty of boating in her lifetime and knew exactly what to do. She unsnapped the plastic window on the side of the boat, jumped inside and started the blower to release any gas fumes from the engine area. She untied the ropes at the dock cleats and started the engine.

"Harry, look " yelled the young man.

Harry Lefler dropped the radio receiver and ran out the door, around the building and onto the docks.

"Hey, lady what are you doing?"

Maggie couldn't hear him because of the storm, but she knew he was running to stop her. She put the boat in gear and took off, leaving the man on the dock waving his arms. She went out of the bay and then headed west to Culebra Island. The storm was blowing with her and made it easier to steer the boat, but the water was still extremely rough and very dangerous. The small boat was sucked into the bottom of swells and spit back up again. There were times when Maggie was sure the boat had left the water and gone airborne.

Lieutenant Harry Lefler went back into the station and grabbed the towel that Maggie had left laying on the countertop. He dried off his head and arms.

"Call the police. We better make a report about this," he told his co-worker.

Chapter 44

They dropped anchor on the fifty-eight foot Hatteras into the bay at the marina on Culebra and launched a six-man rubber dinghy manned with Cuban's men, Turner and Dawson, and the Smiths. Within minutes, they docked the smaller boat at the marina.

"Let's go," ordered Turner.

Mr. Smith helped his wife off the boat. The drenched couple huddled together and walked against the wind, barely able to stay on the dock. Cuban's men followed behind. The two marina workers had gone home when the storm was listed as a tropical storm watch.

The Cuban had made arrangements with an island rental service to have an eight passenger Safari waiting for them, leaving the key in a magnetic keybox under the front fender well. The Smiths sat in the back seat on the way to Mister's house and held hands. Mr. Smith couldn't see any way out of the mess they were in this time, and he was certain they would be killed once they arrived at the house. His only hope would be if they could find a way to make a run for it when the two men with them weren't looking.

Chapter 45

Wells arrived at the Coast Guard Office at 10:05. After hearing the description of the boat thief, he knew it was Maggie Brown.

"You said she wanted to go to Culebra?"

"Yes, that's what she said," the lieutenant said.

Wells thought for a minute, then lowered his head and rubbed his chin. "I'm afraid," he started, "that I'll have to ask for your assistance. I know the weather is rough and getting worse by the minute, but here's the situation."

Wells told the men of the missing girl and about Maggie, Matt, and Bradley. He wanted them to know what they were up against should they choose to help.

"I'll take you there," answered Lieutenant Lefler. "Johnny, you stay by the radio and we'll let you know when we get there and what we need."

"Yes, sir."

Wells and Lefler boarded the forty foot Coast Guard vessel and set out on what they considered an impossible mission, trying to rescue a woman in a small boat during a storm, and if they managed to find her, continue to Culebra in hopes of finding her daughter, Matt Sanford and Bradley. Wells knew an officer on Culebra and would radio him on the way there to meet them at the dock with his partner. The two brave men had no idea of what they would be up against.

Chapter 46

The children made it to the beach, but they were exhausted, injured, and some of them in tears. They collapsed on the beach and Moises was using his inhalator every minute.

"I need to rest," he pleaded.

"Okay, okay." Teodoro gasped for air also.

The children looked at the powerful churning sea in front of them.

"How are we ever going to get your raft to float on that?" Nalda pointed to the water.

Tracey looked at the ragged group of kids around her. She was sure Frieza's arm was broken, Tobias was curled into a ball—afraid of thc water, Moises' inhalator would soon be empty, and Evita clung to her in terror. Somehow, she and Teodoro would have to convince the others they could make it. Tracey had her own reservations. Teodoro was right beside her, sitting with his arms around his knees, looking out into the blackness of the sea. He was used to the rain and ignored it.

"How *is* our raft going to float in those waves?" he asked. The water and its waves were more than he had anticipated.

"The waves are only high at the beach, then the water levels out," Tracey told him. "We won't get on it until we're past the big waves."

Tracey had started swimming lessons when she was three and learned to ski when she was seven. She and her mom belonged to a fitness club with a pool, and they would spend weekends on a nearby lake. She was very much at home on the water and ready to tackle it if it meant getting away from Mister.

"You, Nalda and I can help the others out past the waves, "Tracey explained.

"I don't even know if I can swim."

She could see Teodoro was losing hope. "You'll just have to try," she encouraged. "We've come this far, and this is not the time to give up."

Evita lifted her head and looked at Tracey. "I have to go to the bathroom."

"Okay honey. Nalda, I need the flashlight."

Nalda had shut the flashlight off to save the batteries. She handed it to her. Tracey struggled to stand while holding Evita in her arms. She wouldn't have to take her far to be out of sight from the others on the dark night.

Tracey pointed the light down the beach at eye level and spotted something shiny. She could see the round spot of light from the flashlight hitting against a dark maroon color. As she walked closer, she flashed the light all around the object and could clearly see a boat tucked in a cove.

"I'm going to put you down now, Evita. You can go by this tree."

Evita was afraid, but she had to go so bad she did as Tracey said. They stood beside the cove and while Evita was busy, Tracey waded to her knees to examined the boat with her light. Evita was done in a flash and back in Tracey's arms immediately. Tracey ran back up the beach to the others.

"Teodoro, there's a boat on the beach and the keys are inside."

"Boat?"

"It has the keys."

Teodoro could sense Tracey's excitement. "I can't drive a boat."

"But I can." She smiled and wiggled her eyebrows up and down. She handed Evita to Nalda and motioned for Teodoro to follow her. He examined the boat as Tracey had before, using the flashlight. Tracey unsnapped the side cover and jumped inside. The boat had a V-bow that was completely covered.

"This is the kind of ski boat I use in the summer. What's different is there are two bucket seats and a long bench seat in the back. The boat we used had all jump seats." She plopped down in the drivers' seat. "I can drive this, no problem. And look at this."

Teodoro shined his light where Tracey had pulled a lifejacket from the side pocket. "There are life jackets all along the sides." She counted. "There are six jackets. The other kids can wear these, and this should make Tobias feel safer."

"Are you sure you know how to run this?"

She flipped on the key to activate the battery and watched the gas indicator. "We have half a tank. Let's just get everyone and get going," she said with confidence.

Teodoro left to get the other children. Tracey knew the importance of turning the blower on before starting the boat. She turned it on, then helped the others climb inside. She handed life jackets to Nalda, Freiza, Moises, Juana, Jose, but didn't see Tobias or Teodoro.

"Where's Teodoro and Tobias?" she asked Nalda.

"Tobias won't get in." Nalda pointed outside the boat through the clear plastic windows. Tobias was sitting on the beach shaking his head as Teodoro urged him to get in the boat.

"There are life jackets and Tracey knows all about boats. Look, even Jose is ready to go."

Tobias kept shaking his head.

"You've come this far, and we are almost there."

"Almost where?" he asked Teodoro. "We don't have any idea where that takes us." He pointed out into the dark ocean. "Look at the size of those waves."

Teodoro couldn't argue about the size of the waves. They were huge. The rolling water would form a giant arc in the air and then the tip of the arc would come crashing down upon the beach.

Tracey jumped out of the boat with a life jacket in her hand. "What's the problem?" she asked Teodoro.

"Tobias won't come."

She squatted beside Tobias. "Do you trust me, Tobias?"

"Yes."

"Then I'm telling you my mom and I have spent a lot of time in a boat on the water. I know how to ski, and I know how to swim. This ski vest will keep you floating, and I like you too much to leave you here." She took his arm and tried to put it inside one armhole.

Tobias jerked his arm back. "I can do it."

"Good." Tracey smiled. "Let's go."

Tracey climbed into the boat and looked at everyone. Evita had her arms around Nalda's neck and was against her chest. Nalda was wearing the vest around both of them and they were sitting on the floor. Frieza was sitting on the bench seat in back.

"Does your arm hurt?" asked Tracey.

"The jacket is keeping it tight and it feels better."

Tracey nodded with approval. Moises was sitting between Juana and Frieza. "You can scoot over and give Tobias some room," suggested Tracey.

"Sure," answered Moises as he shook his inhalator.

"What's the matter?" Tracey asked.

"I'm almost out."

Tracey knew he needed his inhalator to breathe and wanted to give him some reassurance. "We're getting underway now, Moises. When we get to land again, we'll make sure you get a new one."

He shook his head and smiled. “I can make it.”

Tracey sat in the driver’s seat. The boat had been put in a small cove away from the rough water next to a clump of trees. It was sitting in knee deep water and tied to nearby trees at the front and back of the boat.

“You untie the lines and throw them in the boat, Teodoro. Then get in,” she instructed.

Tracey started the engine, holding the throttle in the neutral position. Teodoro grabbed the side rails and pulled himself inside the boat.

When the boat started to move, Tobias slid off the seat and onto the floor to sit beside Nalda. The look of terror on his face was clear for everyone to see. His eyes were wide with fear and the white part stood out in the dark against his black skin.

Nalda took his hand in hers and squeezed. “We’ll be all right, Tobias, we’ll be all right.”

Tracey knew the bottom of the boat must be full from the storm, and as it continued to rain, the bottom would continue to fill again. She turned on the bilge pump to release water from inside the boat. Teodoro sat in the bucket seat next to hers.

Tracey put the throttle in the reverse position to back out into the ocean. A wave slapped the boat, spinning it around. She pushed the throttle into the forward position and gave it gas to make it go faster. The boat was being tossed around like a seashell rolling on the beach in the tide. At one point, the prop hit the sand and jerked the boat to a sudden halt. The children sitting on the bench seat quickly slid to the floor to be with Nalda, Evita and Tobias. They huddled together in fear.

Tracey looked around to get her bearings so the boat was headed out to sea instead of inland to shore. The light color of the sand was easy to see, even in the darkness of the night. She had to push the throttle all the way forward to be able to steer the boat in the powerful waves, and to keep them from being pushed back onto the beach.

Laps of water smacked on the sides of the boat, twisting it from side to side. Tracey gripped the steering wheel as tight as she could to hold the boat steady. Waves rushed over the front of the boat as the engine worked to push the boat forward through the water. The children were being bounced around like rubber balls.

Nalda dropped the flashlight when she grabbed the side of the boat trying to catch her balance. It rolled forward and Teodoro stood to get it. A wall of water slapped over the boat, sending it rolling on one side. The boat jerked as it came back down, and Teodoro lost his balance and fell overboard through the open area of the canvas top where the children had boarded the boat. His shoe caught the boat cleat and his head went into the water. He was being dragged along the side of the boat. Moises jumped to help pull him back into the boat.

"I can't get him, he's too heavy," he cried.

Tracey knew she couldn't let go of the steering wheel or shut down the boat or they would be at the mercy of the water. Tobias took a deep breath to gain his courage and went to help save Teodoro. He and Moises used all their strength and were able to grab Teodoro's legs and pull him up from the water and back into the boat. His shoe popped off in the process and flipped overboard. The three boys fell backward with the force of the boat. Tobias hit his head on the boat's fiberglass side.

Holding his chest and gasping for air, Teodoro asked, "Are you alright?"

Tobias rubbed his head. "Just a bump." He smiled at Teodoro.

"Thanks guys." Teodoro took his position back in the bucket seat and looked at the others. Nalda held the flashlight in the air so Teodoro could see she had gotten it. He gave her a thumbs up that Tracey had taught him and held onto the railing on the side of the boat with his other hand.

Chapter 47

Maggie was able to make out the lights at the marina and followed them into the bay. She was tired from holding the steering wheel so tightly. The small boat had taken on a lot of water and the wind had ripped the cover from its snaps on the back of the boat. Maggie's determination had gotten her across the wicked seawater and into the safe harbor of Culebra Island. A few sailboats and powerboats were moored in the bay and she steered around them. Maggie passed a large boat on her way in with the name *Triumphant Force* decaled in gold on the side of it. The size of the boat made her feel insignificant in her smaller boat.

The wind kept her from docking the boat with ease and instead, threw her up against the side of the dock, placing a dent on its side. The boat moved up and down with the rough water. She stretched over the side of the boat to grab onto the cleat on the dock so she could tie the boat to it. After she had secured the front of the boat, she tied the back to the dock also.

Maggie searched around the boat for something she could use as a weapon. She found a small black box containing a flair gun and three flares. She put one flare in the gun and put the other two flares in her pocket. She put the gun in another pocket. She had her sea legs by now and walked up the dock as if the weather was fine.

Looking ahead, she saw a vehicle parked under a lamp pole and saw the Smiths getting into the vehicle with two other men. The men were dressed just as she had seen in her vision. Maggie ducked out of sight behind the marina office. As the eight passenger Safari drove away, it passed a Jeep coming into the marina. The driver left the motor running and the lights on so he could see to walk down the dock to check on his boat. Maggie quickly moved around the building opposite the dock, and when she was near the Jeep, she ran to it, opened the door, and jumped inside. She turned it around and sped away following the Safari. *Now I can add grand theft auto to my list of crimes*, she thought.

Ten minutes after Maggie had gone, Wells and Lefler came into the bay. They used the boat's large spotlight to look around.

"Over there," Lefler said. He held the light on the stolen rental boat. They were moving past the *Triumphant Force* when Wells caught a glimpse through one of the windows, of a man standing below deck. He saw the man holding an assault rifle.

"Wait a minute," he said to Lefler. Lefler put the boat in neutral and Wells used his binoculars to get a closer look. Wells now saw two men dressed in black bulletproof vests, both carrying assault rifles. He knew instantly they were professionals.

"How many men are there?" Lefler asked.

"Looks like just the two."

"Do you want me to try the Culebra authorities again?"

"Yes."

It could have been the weather or just a mechanical malfunction, but whatever the reason, the radio in the Coast Guard vessel wasn't working. Wells and Lefler were unable to make contact with the base Coast Guard station or Culebra police. Just as Lefler was trying to make contact again, the two men on the *Triumphant Force* looked out the windows and saw the Coast Guard boat. They quickly turned out the inside lights.

"That tells us they don't want to be seen," Wells said.

"Do you think they're picking up our radio signal?" asked Lefler.

"It's possible. We need to keep going and follow the Brown woman anyway. She could be in danger. We'll have to come back to this later."

"How do we know where to go and how do we get around if we can't contact anyone?"

"Our only option is to break into the marina office and use their radio."

Chapter 48

"Is there someone following us?" asked Dawson. He was looking in the side mirror.

Turner looked in the rearview mirror and the Smiths turned their heads to look out the back window. Mr. Smith was so worried for himself and his wife, that he was hoping someone was following, even if it was the police.

"We'll just see," said Turner.

He found a driveway and turned in, but kept going so it looked like it was his true destination. If someone was following, they would either pull in now, or come back in a few minutes. He stopped the vehicle and turned out the lights, then waited.

Maggie had been with Matt enough lately and had learned a few things. She thought she had been spotted because she saw the Smiths turn and look at her at the same time. Her headlights were directly on the back window. If they did notice her, they would be expecting her to follow soon and would be waiting for her. She pulled off the side of the road and found a clump of trees to hide behind. Then she waited.

Ten minutes passed and she thought she might have made a mistake by not following them. Just as she was about to pull onto the road again, she saw headlights.

She went unnoticed as they drove past. This time she would stay as far back as she could without losing sight of them.

The Safari turned when they were at Mister's turnoff. Maggie was so far behind, she almost missed them. When she turned, she noticed there was no sign of a driveway, just vacant land. She stopped briefly and turned out the lights, thinking they might have spotted her again. After a couple of minutes, she pressed ahead.

Bright bolts of lightning lit the surrounding area, enabling her to see she was in a remote area. She worried that she might have lost them. Another bolt of lightning displayed the abandoned farmhouse in front of her. She hesitated to go further, afraid the Safari and its passengers were hiding behind the house. She crept forward, and as she got closer she didn't see any cars or people, and drove on.

Another bolt of lightning lit the area again and this time she saw the Safari in the distance. Maggie turned off her headlights and continued in darkness. She was on the hilltop when she spotted the Jeep rental that Matt had taken. *He must be here*, she thought.

Chapter 49

Mama hadn't been able to sleep because of the storm and heard the car doors shut. Turner and Dawson weren't worried about being caught because they had orders to kill everyone anyway, so they parked close to the house. Mama got out of bed quietly so she didn't wake her husband. He usually became irritated if his sleep was interrupted. She walked through the dark house in her nightgown and bare feet.

Turner knocked on the kitchen door and Mama jumped with surprise. They never had visitors. Mister heard the knock and was by her side in an instant.

"Who's there!" he yelled.

No one answered.

"Maybe the storm is getting worse and they're here to tell us to evacuate," Mama whispered.

Bradley awoke to the sound of the car doors. Between his scuffle with Matt and sleeping on the barn floor, he was stiff and sore, and when he stood he heard popping from his knee and ankle joints. He stretched with his arms behind his head, then went to the barn door to peek outside.

He saw the parked Safari and the people at the kitchen door. He was trying, from every angle he could, to make out who they were, but it was too dark. Just as he was about to come out for a closer look, the porch light came on and he saw the Cuban's men and the Smiths. Mister opened the door wearing only his pants.

"Yes?" When Mister saw the way the men were dressed he thought they might have been Culebra authorities and Mama was right.

"Are you Mr. Killbane?"

"Who's askin'?"

"We were sent by the Cuban. I believe you know him," Turner jeered.

Mister was taken aback. "What do you want?"

"We need to talk to you."

"This ain't a good time. How about tomorrow?" Mister started to close the door.

Dawson put his foot on the threshold, "It'll only take a minute."

Turner put his hand on the door and pushed it open. He walked in and the others followed.

Mama left the kitchen and went to check on the children. She went to the girls' room first. When she found the empty beds, she placed her hand over her mouth and gasped. Immediately she went to the boys' room and found that vacant also. Shaking and in tears, Mama went to her bedroom and removed the Parker double barrel shotgun. After seeing that the children were gone, Mama thought perhaps the people in the kitchen had taken her children. She then went to the living room and quietly listened to the conversation going on in the kitchen.

"Let's sit down, shall we?" Turner pointed and everyone took a seat at the table. Mister sat in his usual chair at the head of the table, while Turner, Dawson, and the Smiths sat on one bench seat.

"This is a mighty big table. You must have a family?" Turner asked the question, but already knew the answer.

Mister could sense he and his wife were in great danger and noticed the worried look on the older couple's faces also. Even though Mister's guests were still drenched from the storm, he could see Mr. Smith's forehead was covered with small beads of nervous perspiration by the worried look on his face. He was hoping Mama had gone for the gun, as they had talked about many times in case of an emergency. *Where's the damn dog*, he thought.

Mr. Smith was looking around the room for a way out. If the men would leave to get the children, then he and his wife could run out the back door. He knew it was a long shot, because both men were carrying guns.

Maggie crept along the side of the house keeping as low as she could. She was in back of the house, peeking inside at the edge of the window when she heard the thumping. She spun around and noticed the noise was coming from the outhouse.

Keeping low to the ground, she went to investigate. She could see a board had been propped against the door to hold it shut. Someone or something was inside beating on the door trying to get out. Maggie stood to the side and looked for a small opening to look inside. Matt gave one hard push with both feet and the door flew open. Maggie looked inside.

"Matt!"

"Bert. Am I glad to see you. How did you…never mind. Get me out of these cuffs. I have a key taped to the inside of my belt."

He swung his hip around for her to see. She located the key and opened the cuffs.

"Do you always carry a handcuff key?"

"Never know when it might come in handy, and today it did."

He rubbed his wrists and looked at the bandage on her head. Blood was oozing out from the bottom.

"You bumped your head I see."

"Yeah, I had a fight with a Jeep and I won."

"You might have won that round, but you won't win this one." They turned around and Bradley was standing before them with Matt's gun pointed at them. "You must be a cat with nine lives."

"You're right and I have eight more to go," Maggie said.

"You'll need them."

"You realize those men inside are here to kill all of us?" she asked him.

"They're here to kill the ones inside. I take care of you two."

"And then they will take care of you," she added.

"They're not here to kill me. How do you know about them, anyway?" he asked.

"Let's call it a hunch," she joked, but knew Bradley was not aware of the satire behind that statement. "You seem to know them?"

"That's right. The Cuban, Mister and I go way back. You're a smart woman. Too bad I can't keep you." When Bradley smiled Maggie saw his gold tooth.

"The Cuban is your boss?" Matt was fishing for information.

"Yeah, that's right. He's the mastermind behind the child stealings."

"You steal kids so this guy can have a family?"

"That's where Killbane got greedy. He should have taken the kids for the Cuban, and only the Cuban. But he messed up and took some for himself."

"What does the Cuban do with the kids?"

"You really don't know? You're not as good a detective as Miss Brown here thinks."

He put his hand under Maggie's chin. Maggie slapped his hand away, which made Bradley angry. "He sells the little brats for body parts," he spouted. He saw the look of horror on Maggie's face and liked it. "We get the kids, send them to Cairo, where they cut them up and sell their body parts to the highest bidder. People will pay anything to keep family members alive.

And, after tonight, all the kids here will be sold for parts too, including your daughter."

"You jerk!" With both hands in front of her, Maggie pushed on Bradley's chest as hard as she could. He went sailing backward, the gun went off and he shot a hole through the outhouse. Matt lunged forward, knocking Bradley to the ground. Bradley lost his grip on the gun and it flew out of his hand. Maggie went for the gun. Matt punched Bradley in the face and knocked him out. Matt leaped to his feet, took Maggie by the hand and started running.

"Let's go."

Turner and Dawson jumped when they heard the gunshot and pulled their guns.

"Dawson, check that out," Turner ordered.

Dawson left the kitchen. Turner pointed his gun at his hostages and backed up to stand by the door. At this point he couldn't see Dawson.

Maggie and Matt ducked behind some plants and kept quiet. Dawson was searching near them, using his foot to kick though the tall leaves, and came within inches of kicking Maggie. The wind had slowed, but the rain continued steadily and Maggie felt moisture run down her head and into her eye. When she wiped it away with her hand she felt the sticky blood instead of the rain she expected.

"Who's there?" yelled Bradley as he stood and shook off Matt's punch.

Dawson turned when he heard Bradley and fired his gun.

Bradley ducked when he heard the shot, hoping to avoid being caught by a bullet. When he saw Dawson, he called again. "Hey, it's me—Bradley."

Dawson fired another round in Bradley's direction. Thinking Dawson hadn't heard him, Bradley snuck around Dawson and started toward the house where he thought, once inside, they would see who he was and stop shooting at him.

"We've got to get inside," Matt whispered.

"I believe this is yours." Maggie was still holding Matt's gun and handed it back. He took the gun and slipped the cartridge out, making sure Bradley hadn't tampered with it.

"The children's bedrooms are on the other side of the house," he told her. "We'll look for Tracey first. I'm afraid if the other children see us, they'll be afraid and scream. We'll have to hurry. I don't think we have much time before they take the kids."

They moved quietly, keeping low to the ground. The rain was in their favor this time, camouflaging the rustling they made as they went through the foliage.

Bradley walked through the kitchen door looking at the Smiths and Killbanes sitting at the table. He didn't see Turner standing beside the door.

"Did you manage to do your part of the job, Bradley?" Turner asked.

"Wha..." he swung around and saw Turner. "Oh, it's you. Is that one of your buddies out there shooting at me? That was me outside shootin' at the Brown woman and Sanford," Bradley explained.

"They aren't dead yet? Turner was angry. "Where are they now?"

"I don't know. Out there somewhere."

"You screw up." Turner kept his gun pointed and yelled out the screen door. "Dawson. There's two of them out there, you better get back inside."

Dawson came back immediately.

"You can sit over there with the others," Turner ordered Bradley.

"What's this?" Bradley looked shocked.

"Over there." Turner waved his gun and pointed it to the table. "Give Dawson your weapon."

Bradley took a seat beside the Smiths, never turning his back on Cuban's men. Dawson took Bradley's gun from his holster and shoved it in his belt.

"You're making a big mistake here, fellas," he said.

"No. You've made the mistakes. Our orders are to kill all of you and take the kids. Dawson, go find Killbane's old lady."

Dawson left the kitchen to search the rest of the house.

Maggie and Matt searched all the bedrooms and found them empty, and didn't see or hear the children anywhere.

"Where could they be?" she whispered.

"Maybe they already took them somewhere." He thought for a minute. "We don't have a choice, we'll have to ask. Let's go in through here and surprise them from behind."

Maggie nodded. They crawled through the Killbane's bedroom window and tiptoed over the floor. The loose boards in the hardwood floor creaked and moaned, forcing them to walk even slower so they wouldn't be heard.

The loud blast from Killbane's shotgun echoed through the house. Maggie and Matt dropped to the floor. Dawson flew backward from the gunshot that hit his chest. The power from the gun sent Mama sailing backward. She fell over a chair in the corner, then onto the floor, dropping the shotgun. Mister immediately fell to the floor and slithered around the kitchen opening to the living room to be with his wife. He grabbed the shotgun and helped her to her feet.

The Smiths and Bradley ducked under the table at the sound of the gunshot, and Turner dropped to the floor in his spot. He scooted across the floor as fast as he could, all the time keeping his gun pointed at the people under the table. When he reached the other side of the kitchen, he forced his back against the wall leading to the living room. He was right beside the door opening and could see Dawson lying in a pool of blood. Turner knew the shooter was still around, and now Killbane was gone too.

"Turner, throw me a gun," yelled Bradley.

Turner didn't respond, knowing that if he spoke the sound of his voice would give the shooter his location.

"Come on, Turner, two are better than one," bargained Bradley.

Turner remained silent.

"Damn, Turner. Give me a gun."

Turner couldn't take Bradley's badgering any longer. "Shut up, you fool."

The blast that came next shattered the kitchen wall, hitting Turner in the back. He died immediately, his body slumped in a sitting position on the floor.

"Run out the back, dear, run." Mr. Smith tried to crawl out from underneath the kitchen table and stand, but his knee had given out again. Mrs. Smith was already on her feet.

"Not without you." She tugged at his arm and helped him to stand.

Bradley ran out the door and disappeared into the night. Before Mister had time to load the double barrel again, Matt held him at gunpoint. Mister froze with one hand holding the gun and the other holding two shotgun shells. Matt put his finger to his lips, indicating for them to keep quiet. He twitched his head at Mister and Mama to go into the bedroom. Maggie waited at the door and closed it when everyone was inside.

"Maggie, take the shotgun and ammo from Mr. Killbane."

She did as Matt said.

"Now, Mr. and Mrs. Killbane, where are the children?" Matt demanded.

"Mama?" Killbane wanted to know also.

Mama stood in shock. The look of terror was evident to everyone in the room. Her children were missing and she had just killed a man.

"Mama." Mister grabbed her by her shoulders. "Look at me. Where are the children?"

"Gone." She looked in his eyes. "They're gone. They were gone when I came in to wake them."

Maggie swung her around by the arm so she could see her face. "Do you know what those men came here to do tonight? They're here to take the children to Cairo, Egypt, and sell their body parts."

Maggie began shaking Mama. “Tell me where they went.”

“Maggie.” Matt took her arm and pulled her beside him.

Maggie focused her attention on loading the shotgun and to cool off.

“When’s the last time you saw them?” Matt asked.

“At bedtime,” Mister answered. “We all went to bed at the same time. I didn’t hear a thing until the Cuban’s men showed up.”

Matt was confident he was telling the truth. “Where’s this Cuban guy?” Maggie and Matt asked the same question at the same time.

Mister was afraid to answer.

“You might as well tell me. He sent them to kill you anyway,” Matt told him.

“Miami, he lives in Miami,” Mister answered.

“And is Cuban a last name or a first name?

“I don’t know. He just goes by the Cuban.”

“How many children were here?” asked Maggie.

“Nine.”

“And Tracey, my daughter, is one of them?”

“Yes,” he said sheepishly.

“Where do you think the children could have gone?” she continued.

“I don’t know.”

“Think,” Maggie demanded.

Mama started slowly, “One time, a long time ago, one of our boys tried to leave here. He walked all the way to the ocean. Then Mister brought him back.”

“So they know about the ocean.” Maggie said to Matt.

“The raft,” Matt thought aloud.

“What?” Maggie asked.

“There was a raft in the barn loft. I’ll bet the kids made it.”

“Oh, dear God.” Maggie looked at Matt. “Do you think they could have tried to take the raft tonight?”

Matt knew there was no time to waste. “Let’s go.” He signaled for the Killbanes to go through the door first.

“How’d you get here tonight?”

“I stole a boat.”

“Stole a…okay.” He shook his head. “Where is it now?”

“At the marina. Why?”

“What are we going to do now?” she asked.

“We’ll tie the Killbanes in the barn and take his truck to the marina. Then we’ll use your boat to look for the kids. When the boy ran away before, where did you find him?” Matt asked Killbane.

"On a small beach just north of the marina."

They left the kitchen and walked outside to the barn. Matt looked all around them as they walked.

"What are you looking for?" Maggie asked him.

"Bradley and the Smiths."

The barn doors were open and the overhead light bulb was on, making it easy to see Killbane's truck was gone.

"I guess we don't have to look for them anymore," Maggie said.

"But I doubt if they went together, Bert."

"Do you think this Cuban fellow sent more than two men here?" Matt asked Killbane as he nudged them inside the barn.

"I don't know. Nothing like this ever happened before," answered Mister.

"We didn't wanna hurt the kids. We just couldn't have any kids of our own," Mama added.

Maggie didn't feel any sympathy for the Killbanes. "Let's tie them over here." She held a rope in her hands and was standing beside a barn post.

A gust of wind whipped inside the barn and one barn door smacked against the doorframe. Maggie, Matt and the Killbanes dropped to the floor from the noise. Matt saw the Smiths standing at the entrance and Mr. Smith was pointing a gun at them.

Mr. Smith shot at Matt and Matt shot the light bulb at the same time, darkening the barn. There was more gunfire and shuffling on the barn floor. Then the shotgun was fired.

Silence.

"Matt?" whispered Maggie.

Silence.

"Matt?" she tried again.

"Over here," he whispered back.

She followed his voice, staying on the barn floor all the way. Maggie used her hand to feel for him and found his foot.

"Is that you?"

"Yes."

They remained still in the dark for a moment, listening for any movement from someone else. They heard nothing.

Matt felt around for something he could throw. He found a bucket and hurled it into the air. It hit the barn wall across from them and rattled to the floor. If anyone was still there, he expected someone to shoot at the noise, but no one did. He put his mouth to Maggie's ear. "I think we're alone. Let's make our way to the door."

"I have a small flashlight," she whispered.

"Let me see it."

As quietly as possible, she unzipped her jacket pocket and lifted out the small flashlight, handing it to Matt.

He rotated the end and held his hand over the tiny light beam. There was still no movement inside the barn.

Matt got to his knees, gun pointed, and used the small light to look around. When he was sure it was safe, he got up and then helped Maggie to her feet. He saw the Smiths lying dead at the barn entrance, and the Killbanes were dead beside the barn post. Matt shined the dim dot of light on Mister Killbane. The light wasn't bright enough to see all the details, but Matt could clearly see Killbane and his wife were dead.

"Bert, how did he get that shotgun back?"

"When you shot out the light, he knocked me down and jerked it away. But he only fired one shot, so how did both Smiths die?"

"I shot Mrs. Smith, Mr. Smith shot the Killbanes and I think if we go look, we'll see that Killbane killed Mr. Smith with the shotgun."

"I don't care to look, thanks. Let's just go get the kids."

"Remember, Bradley is still out there, so let's be careful," he reminded her.

They had to walk around the Smiths to get through the barn door and Maggie wasn't about to look down. Matt took Turner's gun from Mr. Smith's hand. He and Maggie headed for the Jeep on the hill.

It was 1:00 a.m. and the worst of the storm had passed through the islands. Rain still came down, but the wind had gone from furious to that of normal storm winds. The temperature had risen to 75°.

When Bradley arrived at the beach and found his boat was gone, and found the raft lying on the beach, he assumed the little brats had taken his boat. He headed to the marina where he would find another boat to use to get back to St. John. He planned to pack a suitcase and disappear with Patty while things cooled off. He would either have to smooth things over with the Cuban or start a new life somewhere. He wasn't worried about starting over, he had been saving money for years in case of such an emergency.

Maggie and Matt took Maggie's rental Jeep and left her "borrowed" Jeep on the hill.

"Where do we start to look for Tracey and the others?" Maggie asked.

"We can start with the section of beach Killbane told us about."

"Matt, how big was the raft you saw?"

"Barely big enough for five children, let alone nine." Matt didn't want to discourage her, but wanted her to be aware of the situation. It was no use trying to shelter her any longer. He could see she was stronger now. Maggie had told him about the events that had taken place at the Rastafarian tabernacle while they walked to the Jeep. He wasn't sure he understood what she had experienced, but he could see how it had made her more confident. In fact, he could see that she was like she used to be years ago.

Chapter 50

All the children screamed when the wind became so fierce that it stripped the boat cover completely off. In some spots the snaps came right out of the boat and blew away with the cover. Once again the children were exposed to the rain. Every time the boat plowed through another wave, it would come crashing down against the water, jolting the children. They cringed with each smack.

"I bit my tongue," cried Evita. Blood ran onto the front of Nalda's shirt.

"There, there now, Evita. Keep your head on my shoulder." Nalda tried to comfort her. She could see the others were frightened too.

"Can you tell where you're going?" Teodoro asked Tracey.

"No, but I've been going the same direction since we left, because the wind is still blowing at us on our right side."

Lightning bolts struck all around them, and with each bolt it was clear to see there wasn't any land in sight. Tracey had studied the maps of the area on their flight to St. Thomas in July. She and her mom had discussed where the islands were located in comparison to Florida and New York. She tried hard to see the maps in her mind.

She remembered St. Thomas and St. John were across from one another and that there were several smaller islands all around them. She also remembered the ferry ride from St. Thomas to St. John had lasted about twenty-five minutes. She wasn't sure how long they had been in the boat, but it seemed to her if she had driven the boat in a straight line, that they should come upon another island eventually.

The wind gusts were farther apart now, but the ocean remained agitated. Tracey was hoping the storm was almost over. Her arms ached from gripping the steering wheel so tightly. She noticed a jerking sensation from the boat, and looked around inside for something that could be causing the movement. The others felt it too and looked at her.

"What's that?" asked Teodoro.

"I don't know." She checked the instrument panel. "I don't see anything wrong."

"It feels like we're running out of gas." Jose said. "My uncle's truck did that once."

Immediately she checked the gas gauge. "Looks the same."

And that was the problem. The tank was at the half way mark when they had left the island and it still read the same. It hadn't moved. She tapped on the plastic cover and the needle dropped to the empty mark.

"The gas tank needle was stuck."

Teodoro's eyes were huge with panic when she looked at him. The boat's engine began to sputter, then it stopped. The children gasped.

Tracey pulled the throttle back, then pushed it forward again, then turned the key in an attempt to start the boat. Nothing happened.

The boat spun around on top of every wave. The children grabbed anything they could find to hold on to and screamed.

Tracey tried to keep the propeller on the engine straight, but she was wasting her time; the ocean was in control.

The small boat was pulled to the bottom of a swell, and the top of a wave sent water rushing inside, completely filling the bottom of the boat. The children screamed with fear. The same thing happened two more times and on the last spin, the boat was forced on its side, spilling the children into the ocean. One last push of water flipped the boat and sent it flying through the air over the children and it capsized.

The children coughed and choked on the water that had been forced into their lungs. The life preservers brought the children back to the top of the water like fishing bobs, except for Tracey and Teodoro. Neither were wearing vests.

Teodoro had hung onto the boat rail as long as he could and when the boat overturned, his wrist was stuck momentarily between the boat and its railing, bending his wrist backward. He heard the snap when the bone splintered. Since he wasn't wearing a vest and couldn't swim, he went underneath the water. He held his breath and tried not to panic, hoping he would float back to the surface as Tracey once explained.

Tracey was an avid swimmer and immediately came to the top. She looked for everyone. "Nalda," she yelled.

"Over here," Nalda choked.

"Is Evita with you?"

"Yes."

Evita rubbed water from her eyes and coughed from the irritation in her throat.

"Jose, Tobias," Tracey called.

"We're right here." Tobias and Jose were beside each other, holding onto each other's life vests.

"Can anyone see Moises, Freiza, Juana or Teodoro?"

"Juana's with me," answered Freiza.

"I'm right behind them," Moises wheezed.

"And I'm behind Moises," called Juana.

"Does anyone see Teodoro?" Tracey asked.

Tracey heard all the "nos" loud and clear. She knew it was highly likely Teodoro couldn't swim and he wasn't wearing a vest.

"Teodoro," she called. She called again, and soon all the children were calling him.

She swam farther away from everyone and called again. The children moved together and tried desperately to hang onto each other, but sometimes the water would whisk one of them away, and then he or she would have to kick back.

Tracey heard someone in the distance. She swam to the sound and found Teodoro going up and down, under and above the water, drowning. "Teodoro, I'm coming."

She remembered what she had been taught in swimming lessons and put her arm around his neck to hold him up and floated backward with him. The choppy water worked against her and yanked him away. She tried again. "Kick your feeet Teodoro."

He kicked as Tracey pulled. "I can stay up on my own now," he said between coughs. "Just pull me to the others." Still overcome by water, he felt better being able to keep his head above the surface.

"I'll take you to the others and you can hold onto their vests. That will keep you floating," she explained.

He nodded and blinked as water slapped his face. When they found the others, Moises was floating on his back and Jose was holding onto the neck of his vest.

"What's the matter with Moises?" Tracey swam to his side. He was floating on his back and wasn't moving, except with the rolling water.

"He was wheezing and holding his chest. Then he threw-up and passed out," cried Nalda. "He must have had an asthma attack."

Tracey put her hand on his cheeks and patted him gently. "Moises, can you hear me?"

She tried to wake him, and when she couldn't, she put her ear to his mouth and nose attempting to hear him breathe, but she was treading water and the laps from the waves made it impossible to do.

"What do we do now?" cried Juana.

"Just hold on to him and keep patting him on his face until he wakes up. We must stay together until morning. Then maybe someone will see us from a boat."

Tracey was trying to give them hope. What she really felt was despair. It would be a long time until sunrise and then she didn't think they would see a boat. The ocean was enormous, and they would be just a speck, even in a group. No one knew they were missing except Mister, and that was her greatest fear, that he would be the one to find them.

Chapter 51

As he approached the marina, Bradley saw Wells and Lefler through the window of the marina, rummaging around inside. He thought this might be a good way to get back in the Cuban's good graces. He assumed Wells and Lefler were on the island to help the Brown woman find her kid. Otherwise, Bradley thought Wells would be at home with his cute little wife watching television.

Bradley also knew that the rest of the Cuban's men would be on a boat in the harbor waiting for the men to return with the kids from the Killbanes. His plan was to take Wells and Lefler to the boat, tell the Cuban's men that the kids were on the ocean in his boat and they could look for them. If Bradley were able to help get the kids for the Cuban, surely the Cuban would see what an asset he was and let him continue working, and let him live.

"Wells." Bradley startled him, but the quick acting officer pulled his gun. Bradley threw his arms up as if he was under arrest.

"Wait a minute, Wells."

"No, you wait a minute. Where's the Brown woman?"

"She's all right. She and Sanford are lookin' for the kids."

"Kids?"

"Yeah, there're nine kids out on the ocean somewhere in my boat. It's a long story, but here's what I know. Ever since the chief's murder, I've been working undercover with the FBI. They didn't want to include you only because they thought the fewer people who knew, the better it would be."

Wells looked at Bradley suspiciously.

"It turns out Killbane and his old lady weren't able to have any kids, so they started stealin' kids for themselves."

"Killbane?"

"Yeah, can you believe it? And Killbane killed the chief because he was gettin' too close to the truth. Tonight we raided Killbane's house to get the kids out. Everybody was there. Killbanes, the Brown woman, her partner Sanford, me, and the FBI."

Bradley could see Wells was starting to believe his story.

"When we got there the kids had run away, and when we got back to my boat, it was gone. So we figure the kids took my boat. And we need you now to help us look for them."

Wells thought for a minute. "What about the Smiths?"

"The Smiths were hired by Killbane as decoys to throw us off track. Make it look like somebody else killed the chief."

Wells could see how the story fit together. "So where are they now?"

"At Killbane's, being questioned by the FBI. The rest of the FBI agents are out in the bay." He pointed toward the water. "We need to get going. Are you with us?"

Wells put his gun back in its holster. He had seen the men dressed in black and realized, because of Bradley's story, that they were FBI agents.

"You stay here, Harry, and keep trying the Culebra police. The storm's letting up and the static should disappear soon and maybe you can get through. I'll go with Bradley," Wells instructed.

Lefler nodded and picked up the radio mike.

"Wells, Lefler can come with us, too. We can use the radio on the boat."

Lefler wanted to come and be a part of the rescue team, but he waited to get his orders from Wells.

"Okay, let's get going then. We've wasted enough time, " Wells said.

Bradley smiled and patted Wells on the back. His plan was working. On his way out, he cut the microphone cord in two, rendering it unusable. They took the Coast Guard boat out to the *Triumphant Force* and drifted beside it.

The Cuban's men had been watching Wells and Lefler since they had spotted them coming into the bay. One of the men came to the side of the boat and looked down. The other guarded from above on the flying bridge.

"Ahoy," yelled Bradley.

The Cuban's man recognized him, but kept his automatic weapon pointed at all three men.

"I need to speak with you," Bradley said, hoping they would give him the chance and not shoot him on the spot.

Knowing he was in control, the Cuban's man allowed Bradley to board his boat. Lefler tossed a line to the man and they pulled the boats together. Bradley stepped on the edge of the Coast Guard boat and up onto the larger boat.

Wells watched as Bradley spoke with the man.

Bradley was waving his hands and pointing out into the ocean. At the end of their conversation, Bradley turned to Wells and Lefler. The man Bradley had just spoken with signaled the other man to come down from the bridge.

"It's okay," Bradley directed. "They want you to anchor your boat here and we'll all go on this boat," Bradley directed.

Lefler wasn't happy about leaving his boat and thought that two search boats would be better than one, but he respected the fact that the FBI was in charge and did as he was told. It only took five minutes to drop anchor and board the other boat, which had worked out well for Bradley. The *Triumphant Force* was leaving the bay while Maggie and Matt were pulling into the parking lot at the marina.

Matt saw the lights inside the marina, but didn't see any people around. He walked inside through the broken glass door and thought someone must have broken it to gain entry into the building. Nothing was disturbed except the marine radio. He picked up the microphone and tossed it back down onto the counter. Matt had been hoping to use the radio to call for help. He scouted around and found an old marine flashlight with a handle. He made sure it worked, then took it with him.

Maggie had already started the boat and was waiting for him at the dock. He hopped on board and they took off to hunt for the children. They were the only two people around and as they drove out of the harbor.

Maggie noticed the big boat was gone and had been replaced by a Coast Guard vessel. "Do you think they're here because I took their boat?"

"Beats me, but it doesn't look like anybody's on board."

"They told me they couldn't, and wouldn't, come out on the water tonight."

"They're here now, aren't they?"

Matt sat on top of the back-to-back jump seats and shined the flashlight ahead of the boat. Back at the dock, Maggie had unsnapped the canvas cover and left it there. Without the top, they were able to see farther in front of the boat. Once they were out of the bay and in open water, Maggie headed north and stayed close to shore in order to see the small beach area Mister Killbane had talked about. Matt aimed the light on the shoreline, looking for anything that might indicate the children had been there.

"There's the raft Maggie, up on the beach."

Maggie looked at the area where Matt shined the light and saw the raft. Matt moved the light along the entire beach hoping to see the children. When he didn't, he told Maggie to head straight out from shore.

Chapter 52

The *Triumphant Force* had made several passes in the area off the northwest side of the island, each time going out farther away from shore.

"What's that over there?" Lefler was using binoculars and saw something just beyond their searchlight.

"Let me see," Bradley jerked the binoculars away from Lefler.

Wells heard the men talking and came to the front of the boat to be with them.

"That's my boat," Bradley said. "But it's capsized."

Bradley signaled to the pilot to slow down. The pilot pulled as close as he could to Bradley's boat without the wake forcing the small boat away. Wells used the spotlight to search the area around the boat, but saw nothing.

"Let's keep looking," Bradley said. "The kids can't be far from here."

Bradley was excited about the prospect of finding the children and turning them over to the Cuban himself. He was sure the Cuban would let him live then. He wasn't aware that once the children were safely aboard, Cuban's men were planning to carry out their original orders, disposing of Bradley, and now—Wells and Lefler also.

A warm breeze blew gently once again, leaving every indication the storm was over, and the ocean was regaining composure.

"Do you see anything?" Maggie asked.

"Something over there." He pointed.

She steered to where Matt was pointing.

"Slow down," he said, and reached over the edge of the boat, pulling the object from the water.

"A shoe," he said, holding it by the shoestring.

"Oh, no."

"Let's look at it in a positive way. They're out here somewhere. Let's keep going."

Chapter 53

"Moises has his eyes open," Jose called for everyone to see.

Tobias was so afraid since he had been thrown out of the boat that he remained totally still, clinging onto Jose's vest. But when he heard Moises had opened his eyes, he had to see for himself. Jose had been holding Moises so he didn't float away, and Tobias used his hands to make his way around Jose to get to Moises.

"Moises, can you hear me?" Tobias asked.

"Yes," Moises said, his breathing normal.

"Boy, you sure scared us," Tracey was by his side.

"Yeah," the others agreed.

"How long have we been out here?" asked Moises.

"Not too long. The storm seems to be about over," Teodoro added.

"It's so dark, but I can see all the stars," Moises said.

All the children looked upward. It was a sky most of them had never seen before. Mama and Mister had kept them inside at dusk and they went to bed most of the time before it was completely dark.

"It's beautiful," said Freiza. For a moment she forgot how painful her arm was.

As all the children looked at the sky, a cloud rolled past and the moon appeared. Gentle "oohs" and "ahs" mixed with the quiet laps of water.

"I hear something," Teodoro said.

"It sounds like a boat." Juana could hear the noise also.

"Shhh." Nalda put her hand up for everyone to be quiet.

They all heard the low rumble of the engine and looked in every direction for the boat.

"Over here," yelled Jose.

"Over here," yelled Juana.

Soon, all the children were calling out for someone on the boat to hear.

"What's that sound," asked Bradley.

Wells and Lefler heard the calling at the same time.
"Sounds like it's coming from over there," Lefler pointed to their left.
Yes, Bradley thought, *it's them.*

Chapter 54

"Matt, I see a light in the distance. See it?"

Matt put the binoculars to his eyes. "Yeah, it's the light from a large boat. Says…Triumphant something on it."

"Triumphant Force?"

"Yeah, that's right."

"That's the boat I saw in the harbor when I came into Culebra. What do you think they're doing out here?"

"I don't know. They must have left the harbor before the storm was over."

"Maybe we should ask them to help look for the children," she suggested.

"If they have a radio on board, we could call the authorities."

She nodded and headed for the boat.

"Help us, help us," the children waved their arms high in the air and kept calling.

Wells couldn't believe what he was seeing; nine children, floating together in the ocean. He wondered how they had survived the storm.

"We're saved." Juana smiled at Freiza and the girls hugged.

The men helped each child on board and the children removed their life jackets and wrapped in the blankets Wells had found on board.

Wells examined Freiza's shoulder and arm while she was still wearing her vest and decided it would be better for her to leave the vest on and keep her arm secure.

The tired, hungry children sat in the cabin, still huddled together, sharing blankets. Wells and Lefler had helped all the children, and Wells wondered where Bradley and the FBI men were during this time.

"Everybody happy now?" Bradley asked as he entered the cabin.

"Is there anything on board we could give the children to eat?" asked Wells.

Bradley was put-off by having to bother with asking Cuban's men for food, so he started looking instead. "Doesn't look like there's anything here."

He was looking in a cupboard when Lefler spoke. "Looks like we have company."

Wells and Bradley looked out the window together and saw the boat lights coming toward them.

"You stay here, and stay down," ordered Bradley, and walked up the short set of stairs. "Never know who's out there."

Wells thought that was a peculiar order. *Who would be out there anyway,* he thought, *that we would have to hide from?*

He followed Bradley, but only made it part way up the steps.

"That's far enough," Bradley said to Wells. He put his gun to Wells' side. Wells looked at Bradley.

"What's this?"

"Just shut up if you wanna keep the kids alive."

"I should have known." Wells shook his head.

"Let's go back down, shall we?"

When the two men reentered the cabin, the children saw the gun and they squealed. Lefler stood in front of the children.

"Everybody on the floor and stay quiet. One little peep and I shoot."

All of them did as they were told. The children stayed in back of Wells and Lefler.

The Cuban's men stood on the side of the boat, one with a flashlight, the other with his hand on his gun.

"Ahoy there!" Matt smiled at the men, while Maggie navigated the boat beside the larger one.

Matt threw a rope to the men and the gunman caught the line. Matt held his hand on the bigger boat so the side of the boats wouldn't rub together. With the light in his eyes, Matt wasn't able to see how the men were dressed. "We're looking for some children," he said.

Wells and Lefler heard Matt, and so did the children. Tracey looked at Teodoro and Nalda, and couldn't help wondering if the man speaking was a good guy or a bad guy.

"The last we knew they were off the east shore of Culebra Island in a boat, possibly about the same size boat as ours. Have you seen anything?"

"We have not." The man spoke with a thick Spanish accent. He then spoke to the other man in Spanish.

"Nada, nada," the other man shook his head.

"Neither of us have seen such a boat or children tonight, señor," he smiled. "But we will keep our eyes open."

Matt could feel something was wrong. "Do you have a radio on board?" he asked.

Maggie sensed Matt's change in mannerism and started looking around the boat. The light inside the cabin was a large hanging marine lantern that put off only a dim light.

"Sí, we have a radio, but it's not working. We could go to the nearest port and notify the authorities for you, if that would help," the Cuban's man lied, hoping to get rid of Maggie and Matt.

"That would be great, thanks." Matt tipped the front of his baseball cap. He took back the boat line and Maggie put the boat in gear and drove away.

"Matt, I saw them." Maggie could barely sit still.

"Saw what?"

"The children are inside the boat. There's a huge brass lantern hanging inside and I saw the reflection of the children huddled on the floor. I think Bradley was there, too, because I saw the police uniform."

"Are you sure?"

"Yes."

"Stop the boat."

She pulled back on the throttle.

"I knew something didn't look or feel right. With those heavy Spanish accents, my guess is those are a couple of the Cuban's men."

"Oh, Matt" Maggie knew that meant the children were in a great deal of danger.

The Cuban's men had radioed the Cuban and reported their status, asking for further instructions. Just as they suspected, their orders were to get rid of the men and bring the children to him. They opened a couple of beers and planned when and how they would kill the three men. They had told Bradley to keep everyone below until he was told otherwise.

Maggie and Matt sat on the sides of the darkened boat and used oars to row back to the *Triumphant Force*. Maggie had reluctantly taken Mr. Smith's gun from Matt, and hoped she wouldn't have to use it. They rowed as close to the back of the boat as they could without being seen.

"We'll have to swim from here," Matt said.

They lowered into the water without making a sound and swam silently to the swim platform on the back of the big boat.

The Cuban's men were sitting on the front part of the boat looking outward sipping their beers.

Maggie and Matt hoisted themselves onto the platform and up into the back of the boat. The cabin door was open, and when they looked inside, they could see the children facing them. Wells and Lefler were still positioned in front of the children, and Bradley had his back to the door.

Tracey looked up just as Maggie peeked inside, and automatically started to say "Mom." She caught herself, covered her mouth with her hand and faked a coughing spell.

Matt pointed for Maggie to go into the cabin and he would head up front to handle the other men. He hated sending Maggie to take out Bradley, but knew he had no choice because he couldn't take care of three men alone. He was counting on Wells to help when he saw her. When Matt was in place, Maggie gestured for Tracey to cough again.

Tracey started coughing and elbowed Teodoro to do the same. He wasn't sure why, but he knew Tracey must have a good reason. Tracey noticed Nalda looking at her mother and coughed out, "Mom," under her breath so Nalda would hear. Nalda started coughing too, and soon all the children caught on and were coughing.

Bradley stood up and barked at the kids. "Cut it out. Shut up." He worried that the children would annoy Cuban's men and desperately tried to stop them.

Bradley saw Lefler glance at something at the cabin door and turned to see what was behind him. As he turned, Wells went for Bradley's legs, causing him to fall backward. His gun went off with the bullet just missing Maggie. She held her position.

Cuban's men jumped and turned around.

"Gently take your guns out and throw them overboard." Matt held his gun on them.

The two men went for their guns. Matt shot one of the men in the shoulder and the force of the bullet made the man twist around and fall overboard. The other man grabbed Matt by the shoulders and jerked him around. Matt took the man's arm and spun him around, twisting his arm behind his back. He took the man's gun out of his hand and tossed it into the water.

Lefler jumped on Bradley, but not in time. Bradley was ready, expecting Wells and Lefler to jump him, and fired his gun. Lefler doubled over with a bullet in his stomach. Wells kicked Bradley's gun from his hand and the two began a fist fight. Maggie waved for the children to follow her. Tracey ran to her and threw her arms around her. They hugged tightly and ushered the other children out of the cabin and onto the deck.

Matt brought the Cuban's man to the back of the boat. Bradley shot one round out the cabin door, aiming at no one. Everyone scrambled to the corner of the boat, trying to get out of harm's way.

"Maggie, keep your gun on this guy's head, and if he moves, shoot him," Matt told her.

Maggie moved Tracey behind her and pointed the gun at the man. She was ready to shoot him if she had to. Matt went, gun pointed, to the cabin door.

"Wells, what's your status?"

"Not so good," Bradley answered. "He's dead. And things don't look so good for you either. Reinforcements are on their way."

Wells and Lefler were dead. Matt decided to try and take Bradley. He threw the handcuffs to Maggie that Bradley once used on him. "Handcuff that guy to the boat and get the kids out of here," he told her.

Matt had hoped to take the children to safety on the *Triumphant Force*, but if what Bradley said was true, and if more of the Cuban's men were on their way, he needed to get the children as far away as possible. Maggie took the Cuban's man to the front of the boat where she handcuffed him to the boat rail, then hurried back to the children.

"We're going into the water now and to our boat, kids," she told them.

"But we don't have our life jackets," Tobias said.

"That's no problem, Tobias," Tracey said. "Freiza is wearing her vest and you can hold onto her."

"I wasn't wearing one and I made it," encouraged Teodoro.

"Come on, everybody, we're almost home," Nalda added.

Maggie could feel the closeness of the children and could see how strongly connected they had become.

"Leonora, will you carry me?" Evita was standing beside Tracey, and from habit had called her Leonora.

"Leonora?" Maggie was puzzled.

"It's a long story," Tracey told her mother.

"And you'll have plenty of time in the future to tell me about it." They squeezed hands and smiled.

Tracey went over the side of the boat and onto the swim platform first. She sat down and lowered herself into the water, taking Evita with her. "Now remember, Evita, don't let go."

"I won't," Evita said, trying to please her.

Once in the water, she was able to help direct the others. Freiza went next, so the children could hold on to her and stay floating. Tracey tread water, but found it more difficult with Evita. When all the children were in the water, Maggie started over the edge. She looked back at Matt who was sitting with his back to the cabin door wall. He and Bradley were at a standoff and Maggie hated to leave him alone.

Matt winked at her, “See you soon, Bert.”

Maggie smiled and lowered herself to the swim platform, then into the water. She led the children toward the Coast Guard rental. Moises was wheezing and Tracey asked if he was doing all right.

“Yes, I’m fine.” He hated giving in to his health and being the weak one of the bunch.

“Asthma,” Tracey answered her mother’s questioning look. Maggie shook her head in acknowledgment. “Freiza’s shoulder is broken, and something is wrong with Teodoro’s wrist.”

“It shouldn’t be too much further, everyone,” Maggie informed them. The water had become calm, and in the distance she could hear the two men’s voices.

“You may as well give yourself up, Bradley. You’re surrounded by dead bodies and in enough trouble already.”

“That’s true. So if I kill you, too, it won’t matter much.”

“You’ve botched things with the Cuban and you know it. There’s no way he’s gonna let you live now.”

“That doesn’t matter either. I’ve got plenty of money to go anywhere in the world and hide for the rest of my life.”

“Yeah? Even the bad guys like to make more money. When the Cuban finds out you’ve taken off, he’ll put a price on your head so high that all the bad guys in the world will be after you. There won’t be any place for you to hide.”

Bradley didn’t say anything, and Matt kept pushing. “He’s probably picked up Patty by now.”

“He doesn’t know about her.”

“Are you that naive? A man like the Cuban knows everything about the people who work for him.”

“He didn’t know about Killbane and his kids.”

“Yeah—but he blames you for that.”

Matt could tell by the tone in Bradley’s voice he was getting angry, and that’s what Matt wanted. He wanted Bradley to react on his emotions.

As Maggie pulled the last of the children on board the small boat, she couldn’t help feeling sorry for the children. She had no idea what they had endured at the Killbanes’, and just a minute ago they had witnessed two shootings. “Tracey, look in the first-aid kit and see if you can find an inhalator or something for Moises.

Tracey started to look for the kit, while the other children found places to sit. Maggie turned on the blower and was getting ready to start the boat when she felt a hand reach up from the water and grab her arm. The hand pulled hard enough that Maggie fell to the side, lost her footing, and fell overboard. The children screamed.

"Mom!" Tracey looked into the water.

The bullet in his shoulder had not killed the Cuban's man and he was trying now to drown Maggie. She managed to yell out to her daughter.

"Tracey, drive away."

Tracey hesitated. She didn't want to leave her mom with that awful man, but did what her mom said. Maggie struggled with the man, kicking and hitting him, but his strength was unbelievable. He kept pushing her head under water. She jabbed at his face with her finger, then remembered his wound. She punched him in the shoulder, and he let go only long enough for her to surface and take a breath of air.

Matt heard the children scream and thought they must be in trouble. Bradley would have to wait. He rolled across the front of the open cabin door, shooting inside the cabin repeatedly. Once across, he leaped up and ran for the back of the boat, still firing his gun at Bradley, then jumped into the water.

Bradley was shooting out through the door at Matt. When he heard the splash, he ran to the back of the boat and fired shots into the black water hoping a bullet would find Matt. Since Matt had always been an avid swimmer, he was well away from Bradley by the time he got to the edge of the boat.

The handcuffed man started shouting immediately. "Get me free from these cuffs, estupido."

When Bradley didn't respond, he started yelling at him in Spanish. Bradley wasn't about to set free the man who had come to kill him. He ran to the boat's control station and readied for take off.

Matt was with Maggie and the man in record time and grabbed the man's neck from behind and squeezed as hard as he could, forcing him to let go of Maggie. She rose to the surface, gasping for air. Matt had lost his gun in the struggle and was forced to fistfight the man.

"Mom, Mom where are you?' called Tracey.

Maggie's throat burned from swallowing the salty water and she was unable to manage more than a squeak. "Here I am," but it wasn't loud enough for Tracey to hear.

Tracey saw the flaregun her mother had put on the dashboard when they had boarded the boat. She held it high above her head. "Duck, everybody."

She shot the gun. The bright flair lit the sky and the surrounding area. Tracey looked around for her mom. She spotted her mom and the two men in the water. She turned the boat around and went back to them.

Bradley saw the flare also. "Thanks," he spoke out loud to himself.

Maggie heard the crack from the man's neck as Matt snapped it. He instantly went still in the water. Tracey had the boat to them immediately and the boys helped Maggie get on the boat. Matt got on and Tracey turned the boat around again and steered away from the *Triumphant Force*. She didn't know where she was going, but she knew it was away from the bad guys.

Bedraggled, Maggie went to the driver's seat and tapped Tracey on the shoulder. "I'll take over, honey."

Matt took the seat next to Maggie's, and the children huddled on the floor. The *Triumphant Force* was a much bigger boat, with twin engines and capable of outrunning their boat. Maggie ran at top speed and headed toward shore, hoping to get there before Bradley caught up with them.

Maggie had one bullet left in her gun, Matt's gun was at the bottom of the ocean somewhere, and Bradley was approaching fast. It was dangerous to travel without the lights on a boat in the dark, but Maggie didn't use them so Bradley would have less of a chance spotting them.

But Bradley was using the powerful spotlight on the *Triumphant Force* and was more determined than ever to find the kids and get them to the Cuban. After what Matt had said about a bounty being put on his head, he knew the only way to appease the Cuban would be getting the children back. He thought once he talked with the Cuban, he would be able to convince him that he had brought him a huge fortune in body parts.

The Cuban's man sat motionless on the front of the boat and stared inside at Bradley. He was ready to ring his neck given the chance.

The passengers in the small boat were unable to hear the more powerful engine approaching over their own motor, but they could see the spotlight coming closer. The children shifted closer to the adults, and Tracey sat on the floor next to her mother, with Evita still clinging to her, in tears.

Maggie thought the young girl wasn't old enough to realize the danger they faced, but was more afraid of the unknown.

Matt could see it was just a matter of minutes before Bradley was on top of them. "Maggie, how well can Tracey handle this boat?"

"As well as I can," she answered.

Tracey nodded in agreement and looked at Matt.

"Stop the boat and change places with her."

"Why?" she asked as she backed the throttle to a stop.

He handed her the freshly loaded flaregun, while she and Tracey traded places.

"Tracey," Matt began, "my name is Matt." He smiled at her. "I'm a friend of your mother's."

She smiled back and said politely, "Nice to meet you, sir."

"Ah, good manners, I like that," he told her. "When I say go, you open this baby up and take off as fast as you can and drive directly in front of the big boat, then turn sharply so we are right beside it and keep going past it. Do you think you can do that for me, sweetie?"

"Sure, I can do anything if I put my mind to it."

"Hey, I like this girl."

Tracey smiled with pride.

Matt focused his attention on Maggie. "I noticed when we were aboard the boat there were two plastic gas cans fastened to the floor of the flybridge. I have one bullet left, and when we go by the boat, I'm going to shoot a hole into the can closest to us. Your job is to fire this flare into that can. The flare should ignite the gas. That should stop him, at least long enough for us to try to get away.

"Okay, kids. I want the younger and injured kids to hide up under the cover in the front of the boat. Let me see." Matt tapped Tobias, Evita and Frezia on their heads. "How about you three."

"I think the girls should hide first, sir," said Tobias. "And, besides, Freiza is already hurt and Moises needs his inhalator."

Moises chimed in next. "I don't need to hide. I can stay with the others."

Matt looked at the faces of the children. "I see we have a strong alliance here. All right then. Freiza and Evita can…"

Before he could finish his sentence, Freiza spoke up. "Excuse me for interrupting, sir, but we've gotten this far by staying together and if it's okay with you, I'll be better off sitting with everybody else."

All the children nodded. Matt smiled at the children. "Huddle closely together then and hold on tight."

Since Evita couldn't be with Tracey, she took the alternative seat with Nalda. The *Triumphant Force* was nearly there and Tracey, Maggie, and Matt took their positions. When Bradley was almost on top of the small boat, he stopped and came to the back of the *Triumphant Force* to point his gun and gain control.

"Go," yelled Matt.

The *Triumphant Force* was still drifting forward when Bradley appeared on the back deck. He held his gun in the air with his right hand. He was surprised when the small boat started toward him and he shot at it, aiming anywhere he could. As the boat sped by him, he ran to the front to get another shot off, but he wasn't fast enough. By the time he got there, Tracey was turning in front of the boat and heading back around it. Matt shot at the gas can and the bullet left a hole near the bottom. Gasoline ran down from the tiny hole and onto the deck.

"Maggie, now!"

Bradley was running from the front of the boat trying to be parallel with the smaller boat and tried to get another shot at them, but he was too late. Maggie aimed the flairgun and fired. The flair was a direct hit and the gas can exploded.

The children ducked and Matt tried to shelter them. Maggie covered Tracey, who kept steering the boat away from the *Triumphant Force*.

Sparks ignited the other gas can and it exploded with flames and sparks covering the entire boat. Within seconds, flames had gotten to the engine room below deck and the main gas tank. The small Coast Guard boat vibrated when the *Triumphant Force* burst into flames.

Maggie took the driver's seat and Tracey hugged her. Tracey then hugged all her friends, who were finally free from danger.

Chapter 55

One month later…

"What time is he coming to dinner?" asked Tracey.

Maggie checked the time on the new watch Matt had gotten her to replace the one she had lost in the Jeep accident.

"He should be here any minute. Did you finish setting the table?"

"Yes, and I lit the candles."

"Thank you." Maggie's mind was on something else. She had planned to talk with Matt about a serious matter, and since they had returned from the islands, things had been very casual and light.

The doorbell rang and Tracey ran to answer it.

"Hi," Tracey greeted him.

"Hi, sweetie." Matt grinned as he kissed Tracey on the top of the head. "How was school this week?"

"Just fine. I got an 'A' on my math test." She took Matt by the hand and led him down the long hall and into the kitchen.

"Great. I knew you could do it."

When they got to the kitchen, Maggie was taking the chicken casserole out of the oven.

"Hi, Bert." Matt looked at Maggie's hair. "Hey, you went back to red."

"Don't you think it was about time?"

"I like the red. What do you think, Tracey?"

"I think the black made her look sexy."

"Tracey." Maggie was embarrassed, but they all laughed. "If you two will take your seats at the table, I'll bring in the food."

"I brought a bottle of Merlot for dinner."

Good, I'm going to need it, she thought.

Matt had been at the apartment enough times in the past month to know where Maggie kept the corkscrew. He took off his jacket and hung it on the back of a kitchen chair and proceeded to open the bottle.Tracey helped by getting two wineglasses, and carried them to the dining room. They sat at their usual seats around the table. Matt poured the wine and Maggie took a long drink. When she set her glass down on the table, she noticed the look on Matt's face.

"I guess I was thirsty," she said. "Tracey, tell Matt what you've been working on all day."

"I'm putting together a party."

"A party? Sounds like fun," he said.

"It's a party for all the kids from the island and their families. Some of the kids I keep in touch with by e-mail and the others, especially Evita—well, her real name is Rachael, I call on the phone. Anyway, I think we should all get together."

"That's a great idea," he said.

"I thought we could do it every year. And since my birthday is in two months, I thought we could do it then. Mom thought we could all meet in Kansas. That way they wouldn't have to travel as far, kind of halfway for everyone."

"That makes sense." Matt looked at Maggie.

"I was hoping you could come, too," Tracey added.

"Well, I don't know about that, sweetie."

"Oh, please!" Tracey bit her lower lip in anticipation. "Mom said it would be fine with her."

Matt looked at Maggie, who seemed to be thinking of something else. She caught his glance. "More wine?" he asked, bottle in hand.

"Yes, please."

"Mom, tell him he can go."

Maggie lifted her eyebrows in a questioning gesture.

"To Kansas," Tracey repeated.

"Of course. All of the parents want to meet you and thank you in person for bringing their children home."

"Then how could I disappoint everyone? Just tell me when."

Tracey jumped out of her chair and hugged him. Maggie finished her second glass of wine, and a third during dinner.

Tracey had plans to spend the night with a neighbor friend, and after dinner Maggie walked with Tracey to Mary's apartment. It was the first night they would be separated since they had come home, and Maggie hated to let her go, but knew it was healthy for all of them to get back to normal.

"Don't worry, Maggie." Mary's mother assured her. "We'll take good care of her."

Maggie thanked her and walked back to her apartment, all the while trying to decide how to handle what was on her mind. Matt was picking out a compact disc to play when she walked into the living room.

"What are you in the mood for tonight? A little reggae perhaps?" he joked.

"Very funny."

He pushed the play button on the stereo and turned the volume low so they could talk over the music as they had many times before and sat beside her on the couch.

"Have you gotten any new cases?" Maggie asked.

"I talked with someone today who's looking for her biological mother. It should be an easy job and won't take me long to do."

"Good, because I have an idea."

"This sounds interesting."

"I want to go after the Cuban."

"What?" He heard what she said, was surprised and didn't exactly understand what she meant.

"It's been a month and no one's been able to locate him."

"He's probably underground and in another country."

"Probably, but what if he stayed close to home, knowing people would think he'd left?"

"Sure, it's possible."

"So, I was thinking if the three of us worked on it in our spare time, we might…"

Matt interrupted. "The three of us?"

"You, Pete, and me."

"Of course." He was getting a kick out of hearing how excited Maggie was about her plan.

"You know, we could keep our day jobs, so to speak. I hate thinking he's out there somewhere, still working his operation and many children could be in danger."

"All right."

"All right? You mean it's that easy? You'll do it?"

"Yeah, why not?"

"Wow." She sunk back into the couch. "I thought this was going to be much more difficult than that."

"Hey, I'm not hard to get along with." He put his arm around her. She responded with a hug.

"Thank you. I've lost a bit of sleep thinking about all those innocent children."

"Is that what's been bothering you tonight?"

"What makes you think something's bothering me?' she asked.

"Ah, let's see. Three glasses of wine in an hour might have been a clue."

She picked up her glass, walked across the room and looked out the window. She could see the busy street five stories below.

"Now that you've committed yourself to working with me, I can take the chance of scaring you off."

"I'm not going anywhere. What's up?" He came to stand beside her.

"I've made mistakes."

"We all have," he assured her.

"Some of them bigger than others, but I'm ready to face my mistakes, make them right—no more secrets."

"Sounds serious."

Maggie took a deep breath. "Tracey is your daughter."

Matt turned and walked back to the couch. He sat and poured the rest of the wine into his glass.

Oh good, he didn't leave, she thought.

"I suspected so," he said slowly.

She turned and faced him. "I'm so sorry, Matt—for not telling you sooner. Every time we talked about children years ago, you were so emphatic about your feelings and said you didn't want children."

"That was so many years ago, and we were so young."

"Yes, but you said it anyway, and I knew someday I would want kids. So I made my decision to leave. And I was pregnant and didn't know it."

He thought for a minute. "Then you were pregnant at the class reunion?"

"Yes. I was going to tell you then, but just couldn't find the right time or the appropriate words."

He played with his glass. "She's a beautiful girl."

"Yes, I know."

"Does she know?"

"To tell the truth, I think she suspects, or she wishes you were her dad. In the past month she's become very attached to you. I haven't told her, I thought we should do it together."

"You know I love her? She's so infectious."

Maggie smiled, walked to the couch and sat on the edge beside him. "What do we do now?"

"I'm not sure. We tell her, of course."

Maggie nodded.

"I love you, Maggie Brown."

"You told me so a month ago."

"And you said then, you still loved me."

"Yes, I do."

"I still have your ring."

"What are you saying?"

They looked into each other's eyes.

"I'm saying we've wasted enough time, Maggie Brown. We've wasted half of our adult lives." He took her hand. "I'm saying we should get married."

Maggie smiled. "We probably should."

Printed in the United States
84098LV00004B/79-84/A

9 781424 172573